3ENOUTH
COLE

HOMO THUG

BY

Asante kahari

Zenobia
Cole

HOMO

THUG

Black Print Publishing Inc.
4511 Avenue K
Brooklyn, and NY11234

ISBN 0-9748051-6-5

This and many other titles Published by Black Print Publishing Inc. may be purchased for educational, business, sales or promotional use. For information please write: Marketing Department, Black Print Publishing Inc

Published in 2005 by

Black Print Publishing Inc.
4511 Avenue K, NY 11217

Acknowledgements

There are so many people that I must thank that the pages of this book simply could not contain them all. Good and bad, negative and positive, there are so many people who contributed to the success of this project. There are a few who stand out and for that I must give them their rightful due.

To Dexter Brathwaite President of Black Print Publishing Inc. Thanks for the opportunity you provided by making this dream a reality. To Denise Campbell Executive Editor at Black Print Publishing, this book truly would not have been published on such a grand scale had it not been for you. I am eternally grateful for your support and guidance.

To Ms. Francine Shelton, I know it is hard for you to show me how much you care for me because it would seem like choosing sides between other family members but you have shown me in more ways than one that you were down for me and your daughter Pat. I will never forget your love and support. Trumayne, Ava, and Jordan, you have truly filled the void of losing my daughter. I know at times it seems I don't care, it's just a front, I love all of you. Jarrel, your just a brother from another Mother, I know you like me too, stop frontin. I would never take Pat from you we both love her too much.

To my Aunt Joyce, God knows I want to do something good for you, you stuck by my side through every bid, you are truly the only mother I will ever know and if that hurts my real mother so be it, its the truth. Jeff Sledge, Jeff Capers, Murder Mike, Boogie, Stan Rob, Troy, Trick, Big Phil, Herb, Keith, Salon 804, Johan Bailey, Bilal, Red, Otis,

Reggie, little Robert, Sean Potlow, Chico, AZ, Jab, Lukemon, Akmire, Damon, Spanish Randy, Little Troy (my brother from another mother).

In case I forgot anybody out there Gangster Shout Out to my whole Harlem Family. My uncles, Kenny and Nate, My Aunts Tricia and Linda and My Nieces Destini, and Alec. The Daniel's. My brother's Jr and Danyule. My sister Jillian and my family in Guyana, I'll be home soon Georgetown - Berbice Mafia. My twin brother's in England one day. I love you all dearly. Last but not least, to the two most important females in my life. My daughter Octavia Nicole Kahari and Patricia Dyan Harris. My love for the both of goes deeper than any ocean, as round as any cup, all of the Mississippi could not fill it up. Pat, you have stuck by me when no one else would. You allowed me to pursue my dreams full speed ahead. When I was dead broke with no pot to piss in nor window to throw it out, you shaped this clay into a work of art. I hope that the breath of life remains in me long enough for me to show you just how much I appreciate you. When all others told you to forsake me, you showed them that love conquers all. To all of those who did not believe I want to thank you as well, your negativity was an instrument of perseverance. I guess I prove all of you wrong. I will not waste my breath in naming you, you know who you are. That hurts more than anything in the world, to not even be acknowledged. While you are hurting, we are healing. God bless! The last word must be reserved to you my dear. I love you with all my heart. Patricia D. Harris.

CHAPTER ONE

"Count time, count time. I need to see all of your swinging dicks out on deck." That was a call over the P.A. system for all inmates to appear for a headcount before the next shift of correctional staff took over. The count was nothing unusual to me. After all, I had spent well over five thousand four hundred and seventy-five days participating in one count after another, being on the last leg of a fifteen-year sentence for a robbery gone bad. The victim was no older than I was. I decided if he wasn't going to give up his V-bomber coat, then I was going to make sure that he wore it at his funeral.

I was finishing up my bid at Sing Sing, a maximum-security prison located in Ossining, New York. The prison was in the middle of nowhere. A small town with nothing but ol' crackers who spent their days as farmers, and longshoremen when the Hudson River was bustling with traffic and commerce. I lived in a community of about twenty-three hundred inmates, mostly blacks and Hispanics (the rest were a hodgepodge of whites, Asians, and a few East Indians).

There's a uniqueness to the prisons in New

York and California a diversity of races and ethnici-
ties that make for a boiling pot of mayhem and chaos
amongst the inmate population. In prison there is
always something to fight about, be it drugs, personal
property, phone time ... or the shortage of fags
parading their goods up and down the tiers.

I was fifteen when I caught my case and sixteen and a half when I finally got transferred to an
adult facility. I stayed at Sparford until my sixteen
birthday; it took an additional six months for me to
be transferred upstate. I had never been with a
woman, prior to my sentencing. I had girls; I just did-
n't fuck any of them. I was too busy in the street for
that.

I'm glad I was prepped for prison by going to
Sparford. That youth detention center was nothing
more than a glimpse of what prison life would be
like. Unlike prisons, detention centers like Sparford
were designed to feel like a home away from home.
They gave you responsibility by allowing you to lock
and unlock your own cell doors.

I tried to stay away from the masses as much
as possible, rarely going into the recreation room. I
wasn't trying to get caught up into the shit that my
counterparts were into. With some of the things going
on behind its walls, you would think Sparford was an
adult prison. Some of the female counselors would
take a liking to the more mature-looking detainees.
On any given night, you could catch a female counselor in some young boy's cell teaching him about the

facts of life. Most of the boys knew more about the birds and the bees than the women themselves. I think because the women couldn't get a man on the street they were always ugly! they had to come into the kiddie jail to fuck with some young boy not yet old enough to shoot puppy water out of his penis.

The detainees were no better, in some respects. With nothing but testosterone running through their veins and no little girls to afford them the opportunity to express their male prowess, they were left to practice on themselves. It was not unusual to catch younger and weaker prey being violated in the janitors' supply room by the gym. The bigger boys would force the younger boys to keep watch for counselors who might realize heads were missing in the gym until it was their turn to be violated. I felt sorry for them, but what could I do? I was no match for most of them. Shit! I had my own ass to worry about. My body was just taking shape. By all accounts, I was pretty well-defined for my age. I always had a six-pack and my muscles were compact, so I looked bigger than I actually weighed. I could take on most of the kids there with no problem, but against the mob, I am nothing. The troops would always rally against dissenters, no matter how big or tough they were. You had three choices: mind your business, participate, or condone it. I chose to mind my business; in essence, all I was doing was condoning it.

Robert Saxon was the biggest motherfucker at Sparford. He could crush the life out of you if he got his hands around you. We called him Tislam. (His older brother, a "five-percenter," gave him the name.) Every time he spoke he would foam at the mouth. I would venture to say I have yet to see a nigger as ugly as he was. I can see why those young, tender, little babies would scream they couldn't bare the thought of him kissing all over them. I know he used to kiss them in the mouth because I busted him once when they moved all of us in the gym while they did construction on all of the cells. We were housed in the gym for about sixty days. The worst sixty days for all of the little boys being abused.

Tis was so blatant with his shit. He would wait until the lights went out and the counselors were in their office. Then he'd take his favorite little Spanish cutie, Rico, whose long hair made him look just like a little bitch, to the back of the gym where the bunks created a semi-partition. Tis would make Rico get on the bed and turn his face toward the pillow while he penetrated him from behind. Rico got so used to it, he didn't even bother to scream anymore. (I think he felt like he was safe in some respects. He knew that as long as Tislam was fucking him he didn't have to worry about anybody else robbing him of his dignity and self-respect.)

Tislam, a sixteen-year-old predator with nothing to lose and no one to love him, didn't share Rico the love of his life with anybody. In and out of Sparford since he was eleven, Tis would be on his way "up north" in a few months, and he knew he

4

would be there for a long time. Like me, this was his last go-around as a juvenile.

He was sentenced to ten years for dragging a woman to her death while trying to steal her Renault Alliance. When he pushed her out of the driver's seat onto the ground, her coat got stuck in the car door and, as a result, she was dragged-at top speed-for damn-near five blocks before the police caught up to him and released her lifeless body from the car. His mamma had had it, so he was pretty much all alone. His brother, meanwhile, was doing twenty-five to life for killing his uncle over stealing his drugs.

Tislam never saw anything wrong with what he was doing. To him it was just the way things were supposed to be. I mean, on a deeper subconscious level, he must've known there was something wrong with what he was doing but, under the circumstances, he was able to rationalize all of it.

After watching the goings-on around there for so long I began to get numb to the situation myself. It didn't disgust me as much as it used to, a sure sign of becoming institutionalized. That numbness just creeps up on you like a thief in the night and, before you know it, what is completely abnormal becomes normal to you and what is normal seems to be abnormal.

A few times I had been invited to partake in "trying the goods," but I refused every time, not because I thought it was beneath me but for fear that I might just like it and become addicted to it. The last thing I needed was to give in to my carnal desires like Tislam did. I wanted to fuck bad; I just didn't want to fuck any boys.

Convinced it was the love of a female touch I was missing, I knew my yearnings were misdirected and would wrestle with those feelings many a day and night. The only way I could suppress my hunger for the feeling of flesh against my flesh was to jerk off. Every chance I got I made sure to release my frustrations out onto the floor of the bathroom. "Sally and her four sisters" would feel my rage and insatiable lust for the touch and warmth of the opposite sex. Sometimes I would jerk off so much I would not have enough strength to make it through the rest of the day.

I knew that on the state level the goings-on around me would be far worse than anything I could possibly imagine. Tis would have no problem fitting right in. After all, he was an animal with a savage upbringing. The only thing I was prepared for was the fact that I might lose my life trying to protect my most prized possession-my ass. I figured it would be better to go all out and die for the cause rather than just give it up willingly and be a victim for the duration of my bid. I wasn't about to live like a bitch, being bartered out for goods and services by every swinging dick in the joint.

I had heard through the grapevine (from my guidance counselor) that Tislam, a few others, and myself were going to be transferred to a state facility the following week. I was told to call my family and alert them of my relocation. I hadn't spoken to my mother in a minute. We had nothing to talk about. She was not feeling me, an embarrassment to her good Christian name. Nonetheless, I called her, anticipating what she was going to say before the connection was even made.

"Hello, Ma, it's me...Michael."

"Hey, what made you call?"

I didn't know I needed a reason, I thought to myself. "I'm being transferred upstate very soon and I wanted to call you to let you know what was going on."

"Well, call me when you get where you're going. I hope you are getting God in your life. Jesus is the only thing that is going to help you out of your situation."

"Well, anyway, I gotta go. It's feed-up time. Tell Shanel I said hi."

"All right," she responded, "I will." I hung up the phone and headed back to the makeshift dorm in the gym to prepare for feed-up.

* * *

I should have known she didn't care. In all her glory, she had the appearance of a loving mother, a bona fide, holy-rolling Christian, who waited and trusted in the Lord for everything. Everyone in my projects thought she was a saint. Always on the move, you rarely saw her without church regalia on. I called her "the devil in a red dress."

She acted like a Christian in the street and at church, but that was as far as it went. At home she was more like a demon. Me and my sister would get beatings for no reason. My mother was dealing with a lot of personal issues and I think the only way for her to deal with those demons was to pretend that those demons were lodged within me and my sister's body and try to beat them out. At least, that's what I'd like to believe-it would explain our suffering a little better.

Physically, she was not a pretty sight to look at. On a scale of one to ten, I would have to say she was a one-and that's pushing it. You know she was ugly by the mere fact that it's one of her own calling her so. (This was one of the things that me and my sister always agreed on-my mother's ugliness. Amazingly, my sister and I were good-looking...considering. I guess it's true what they say: Two ugly people will make beautiful children.) She had a terrible case of permanent acne. My aunt told me that, as a child, my mother would bust the bumps repeatedly until they became small scar tissues that formed colloidal-like craters. To add to that, she was a plump heifer with no shape.

Outwardly, she was the cleanest woman you would ever want to meet. She stayed caked-up in make-up, making it damn-near impossible to tell that she hadn't bathed in three or four days, the funk hidden deeply beneath the ounces upon ounces of perfume she would spray on as a top coating to mask her foul odor. My mother, "queen of the birdbath," also had a habit of biting her nails. This made her hands look disgusting. I had always thought that my mother was hurting from the pain and insecurity of abandonment by her own mother.

My grandmother had come to the United States from what was then British Guiana. She was granted a visa to be a nanny for some rich white folks in New York City. (My mother was about six or seven at the time.) She had promised my mother that she would return for her as soon as she got settled. She never got settled. My mother would run into her mother ten years later at a Brooklyn Macy's department store. (My aunt was the one who recognized her.) When they confronted my grandmother-the mother of three boys and three girls-she tried to make a dash for the door. My mother's life hasn't been the same since.

After that fateful meeting in that department store, it took many years for my mother to come around to talking to my grandmother and allowing her to see her two grandchildren. I can't say it improved things for us-her bitterness was just too strong. She won't admit it, but she had become the very thing that she herself had despised-an uncaring mother.

*   *   *

I couldn't deal with the pain of someone not caring for me. I wanted desperately for my mother to reach out to me. I wanted to hear that she had my back and would be up to visit me every chance she got. I knew I would be leaving Sparford in a matter of days, yet I couldn't summon the courage to ask her to come visit me this one time while I was still in the city and just a train ride away. That hurt would never go away, and I had no outlet, to get it off my chest. What was I going to do, break down in prison?-no way. After I got off the phone with her that day, I knew what life would have in store for me. I knew that life meant nothing if the woman that brought you into this world didn't give a damn.

Prison meant nothing to me now. I needed to be more like Tislam at this point. His "strength" came from understanding and accepting that no one gave a damn about him, and if I was going to survive the rest of my days behind the wall, I needed to do the same thing: Put on my game face and suck up what-ever life was going to throw at me behind these walls and outside of them as well. I made a pact with myself that I was never going to allow my heart to be broken again.

From that moment on, I would accept my fate

and become just as cold as the next man. I was going to act like a savage like everyone else and show neither fear nor mercy. I started to see wrong as right and right as wrong. What Tislam was doing wasn't as bad as I thought it was. After all, boys needed love, too. I made up my mind that if the opportunity ever presented itself again for me to get in on a "piece of the action," I was going to accept it graciously, rationalizing that I would never do it on the street and that prison was as far as I was going to let it go. I had a lot of time to do and a lot of frustration to release. What better way to release my frustration than the "good, old-fashioned way"?-the only difference was that this person would have a little bit more hair on their body than the average female. It didn't matter to me. I had made up my mind. I would pitch, but I damn sure wasn't going to catch.

CHAPTER TWO

Weeks had passed, and today was the day that Tislam and I-the only ones being transferred-would be moving to a maximum-security joint upstate. My counselor informed me that we would be going to Sing Sing, in Ossining, New York. We were allowed to walk around the facility and say our good-bys while waiting for the bus. I didn't really have any-body I felt I needed to say good-by to-this was jail, not the army.

Of course, Tis made good of the time by pay-ing a special last-minute visit to Rico. It was a very emotional moment for him-he really did love Rico. (They had a bond that only the both of them could understand.) At any rate, they went into one of the cells under repair, Tis simply throwing a sheet on top of the cell door and letting it drape down to the floor. I wasn't trying to be nosy-who am I kidding?-but, from outside the cell door, I could hear them kissing.

Curious, I moved the makeshift curtain ever so slightly. You had to see to believe. They were like newly-weds strolling through Central Park, with goo-goo eyes and shit. Tis floated his fingertips gently through the open spaces of Rico's hair, finely cornrowed and greased to perfection. They began kissing as if they were in some Hollywood movie production where the love scene set the tone for the whole movie. Tis was so passionate when it came to making love to Rico. I couldn't believe this motherfucker had that kind of feeling for this nigger. I think he would have killed concrete for that little Spanish red pepper.

Infringing on their most intimate of moments, I felt out of place, but I couldn't care less-I was too into the craziness of it all to mind my own business. Tis stuck his tongue in Rico's mouth and they began to exchange oral fluids. As they pecked each other, I began to play love songs in my head to the rhythm of their kisses. I couldn't be certain whether Rico was acting to protect himself or was really enjoying his relationship with Tis. One might argue he was just doing whatever it took to survive, but the way they touched, caressed, and fondled each other was all too intimate for it to be one-sided.

The two of them made me question the very nature of love itself. All of a sudden, love didn't make much sense to me anymore. (What did I really know about love, anyway?) Could I be overlooking some-thing that I should be paying attention to? Is love just between a man and a woman, a boy and a girl? I felt like it could only be explained by me experiencing it for myself. That moment in time didn't make it any easier for me. It was all too confusing and fucked up for me to think straight.

Just then I could hear the counselors calling for

both me and Tis over the loudspeakers. It was time to roll out. I could hear Tis saying to Rico in the cell, "I am going to write you as soon as I get up north. I hope I get a chance to see my brother while I am up there. I want you to take care of yourself ...and don't let none of these punk motherfuckers front on you, you hear me?"

Rico responded with a nod of agreement. He looked like he'd just lost his best friend or childhood pet. I think he was just afraid of being somebody else's bitch after Tis left. He knew he didn't have the courage to refuse a nigger. He also knew that life would be business as usual for him. The life of a "forced fag" in the joint is one of misery and dread.

I decided I had seen and heard enough and began to make my way down the hall, leaving them to finish up their parting ceremony. A female counselor then informed me that our transportation was outside and that I should gather my things. What things? I didn't have much. My mother didn't care, so it wasn't like I had pictures, a lot of clothes, or anything else. I had a few cards that I had made myself and pretended they were sent to me by my mother, and a crucifix I had made in arts and craft class.

Tis had more shit than me, most of which he took from other people. I would always sit in judgment of him and the relationship he had with his family when instead I should have been looking at the relationship I had with mine. On a jail level, he was doing better than good, living better than in the street. I could see why he didn't mind being locked up-this was the one place where he felt like he was important.

I went to my bunk and put together the little shit I had in a sheet: a few bars of Lisa soap with lye, a toothbrush, comb, a few pair of white, state-issued underwear, three pairs of socks, my Zulu Nation beads, and a Bible. I laid the sheet on the floor and threw everything in before tying it in three knots. I only had one pair of pants and two white T-shirts that I knew wouldn't last. I didn't want to wash the same pair of pants and shirt everyday. Why should I have to do things that "Herbs" do? That weighed heavily on my mind. A part of a nigger's respect in jail comes from how he looks in the penal. It sounds sick, but it is true.

Most of the so-called gangsters in jail don't want to look busted and will prey on the weak, their rationale being, "Why should I have to suffer when this mother is in here fresh to death and can't hold his shit down?" I never really saw it that way until I packed my shit up. I mean I was holding myself down and didn't have problems with anybody. No one ever tried me, either because they knew better-what I'd like to believe-or, more likely, because I did-n't have shit to take. Besides, I wasn't having it and niggers knew that.

I didn't know what to expect in an adult joint, except it would be far worse than this. I had heard a lot of rape stories on the street that made what Tis was doing seem like child's play. I knew I had to "man up" and do it real fast.

I took a slow, deep breath and recited to myself, "Fear no nigger, and trust no bitch," trying to build a level of confidence and resistance to fear that would go unchallenged.

Transforming into a tough guy but not fully there yet, I had to play the part until I could be that-at will. You had to see I wasn't having it from the first time your eyes made contact with my face. I wanted to be as hard as the prison walls, just making sure my game face would suffice until I was up for whatever, whenever.

The state transportation bus, beeping loud and alerting everyone within a few hundred feet of its presence, had just rolled into the un-loading and re-loading area. Blue Bird (written across the front) was a prison on wheels. It had gates on every window to remind me that I was going nowhere.

Without being told to do so, I made my way to the front of the administrative gate to prepare to get shackled to get on the bus. They were calling for Tis over the P.A. system and he wasn't acknowledging-for whatever reason.

Three menacing state guards came to chaperon us to our new home upstate. They must've seen it all upstate, I thought. They looked like they spent all of their days and nights at the weight pile and wasn't about to take no shit from two young punks…mother's milk still on their faces.

Tislam came prancing up to the gate with his bag-like he was going away on an adventure or something. The guards didn't look too happy with his disposition. I was thinking to myself, If he had any sense, he better get his act together real quick. I had heard stories about correctional officers finding creative ways to make life a living hell for troublesome inmates. I wasn't trying to piss anyone of them off.

One of the guards took center stage with a clipboard in his hands. "My name is Officer Bogart Shelton. When I call your name, take a step up and answer like you got a pair. We can make this as easy, or as hard as you want it to be. Both of you will be around in the system for a long time, so it would behoove you to listen when advice is given to you; it will only be given once." He looked at the board. "Robert Saxon, " he said in a loud voice.

"Here," Tis mocked loudly.

"Step up. Extend one foot out at a time and let one of my officers put the leg restraints on you." One of the officers motioned for Tis to come to him to put the leg braces on.

"Michael Fraser."

"Here, sir." Not wanting to come off like Tislam, with his unflattering sarcasm, I had to throw the "sir" in, to let him know I had respect for him.

He motioned for me to let the other guard put the restraints on me. Tight and pressed cold against my ashy ankles, I saw them as "shackles." Prison is truly a form of slavery, I thought-you have free labor, a racial divide, and a taskmaster. Now I knew how those first slaves felt as they stood on the auction block waiting to be sold to the highest bidder.

First it was the shackles, and as if that wasn't enough, then handcuffs. The guards placed a black box-like a covering-over the handcuffs, so we couldn't move our hands in either direction.

(Ironically, the black box was created by an ex-con who had served all of twenty years in Attica for rape and murder-leave it to an ex-con to invent a device to lessen a nigger's chance of escape and make the police rich at the same time! The dumb ass designed the box while in prison and showed it to a prison official. Unbeknownst to him, the prison official patented the black box and the rest is history. Just too eager to help the man...the ex-con died penniless in a YMCA two years after his release.)

The upstate bus came every couple of weeks, so I figured we would be making a whole lot of stops along the way to pick up other prisoners in other city and county jails who had been sentenced to state time.

Me and Tis, the first to be picked up for the trip, were herded on the truck like cattle and placed in seats apart from each other. There were chains connected to every seat bottom, and our ankle cuffs were locked to the chair chain so that if we miraculously got out of one chain-or both, for that matter-we still had to uproot a steel chair to go anywhere. This was going to be a long ride, I thought.

I really had no concept of how far I was going. I had never even left the five boroughs. To me upstate was a thousand miles away. When old-timers came home and told jail stories, they would mention being in the mountains upstate. The closest thing I ever saw that resembled a mountain was the huge solid rock in Mount Morris and Central Park.

The bus pulled off. I was going to be missing out on a lot of shit being locked away in the man's chicken coop. This would be my last view of the city for a very long while. The sun beamed on my face through the gated window as I gazed at children playing in the park and birds gliding gracefully from one light pole to the next. All of a sudden I became aware of the value of life and just how much my freedom was really worth.

The hustle and bustle of the noisy city streets played like a symphony to my ears as cars honked and common folk screamed obscenities at cab drivers. I could feel the rhythm of life with each beat of my pounding heart. I felt like my heart was connected to the pulse of the city. The farther I got away from it, the fainter the beat would become-as if the life was being sucked right out of me and I would die the moment I stepped foot into the joint.

As we stopped at city jails in every borough,

new faces emerged, changing the demographics in the bus. Some looked like they had made the trip on several occasions before, others looked like it was going to be their last. Their eyes pierced through the cold steel windows as if they were being fed their last meal on death row. Funny how a man's spirit can be broken by the simplest of things, I thought-the rustling of the trees, the sound of life buzzing right before you. I guess it all depended on which side you were viewing it from.

From the seats we were in, our view was one of despair. How could life have come to such a head for me? In my wildest imagination I would have never dreamed this for myself. I had to stop thinking for a moment, free my mind of reality. The reality I didn't want to deal with or accept. But the only thing for me to do to help me make sense of it all was to think about what I had done that landed me there in the first place. I had to see I was no more or less than anyone on the bus.

Here I was being judgmental of the other prisoners on the bus and my crime was probably worse than theirs. I was afraid of their faces when I should have been afraid of my own. I had killed a person-a little boy with a life, family, and dreams, just like me-because I had coveted what he had. He would never be able to make good on his dreams because of me.

I realized there was no need being a bitch about it now. If I was man enough to snuff someone's life out, then I had to be man enough to accept that it might just happen to me, too. Not until that moment did I really believe I was going to be okay and that, as long as I accepted the reality of death, there was nothing to be afraid of. I couldn't bring him back, so I might as well roll with the punches. I was determined to be as tough as any man that crossed my path-if not tougher. As we got on the Major Deegan Expressway I tried to shake off all the fear and timidity and replace it with an armor of courage.

The only thing I was concerned about now was when I would see the streets again. I was young, so I knew it wasn't going to be forever. I wasn't sure how old I would be when I hit the bricks again. I figured, at worst, thirty-if they made me bring that five to fifteen to the door. Not bad, I thought. I would still be young enough to have kids and be able to play with them. More importantly, I would be young enough to still have a life and old enough to know what to do with it.

As we passed by the highway signs and exits I began to wonder how everything would look when I got out. I tried remembering all of the landmarks on the side of the highway. That way I would know if they changed when I hit the bricks again. The Stella D'oro bread factory was on Exit 5 on the opposite side of the highway. I could smell bread baking through the window, my mouth forming an ocean of saliva. Loehman's Clothing warehouse stood a few hundred feet away from it. I marveled at everything I saw. I had so much to appreciate and so little time.

It is amazing what we grow to love and adore when those things are taken away from us, I thought- the breeze that climbed on the bus through a crack in the window, the whistling of the trees. It was all priceless to me. Unfortunately, I didn't know how much. So that I wouldn't get too emotional about it all, I closed my eyes and went to sleep, awaking when the bus came to a complete stop.

CHAPTER THREE

I was awakened by the bright glare from the spotlights that hung high in the air above the loading and un-loading dock, the fluorescent lights almost blinding me. It reminded me of the heavily lit interrogation room at the police precinct. The brightness of the light and the heat that emanated from it would have elicited a confession in about two minutes flat from the most hardened criminal.

Officer Bogart Shelton instructed everyone on the bus to relax because only two people were getting off at this stop. He called out my name and Tislam's and told us to wake up because he would be unchaining us in a minute. There were about four other buses loading and unloading inmates, each bus a circus of minorities young and old.

The building alone was enough to send fear through a man's veins. I could tell by the structure that we were in the big leagues. The walls of the prison, spanning upward as far as the eye could see, were massive. The concrete appeared to be so thick it looked like it could take more than a thousand years with a bulldozer to penetrate it. On each side of the building was an encased tower made of more concrete and bulletproof glass from which an officer with a double-barreled shotgun looked out menacingly. There was definitely no chance of escaping this joint.

The bus was sandwiched in-between the concrete wall and a twenty-inch steel door enforced with a five-inch bolted lock that could only be opened with a key from one of the guards in the tower above. And the only way to obtain the key was to go to the main tower and request it. After a series of test questions the main tower would instruct the other tower to let the key down in a bucket. In other words, if you were lucky enough to steal an officer's uniform, you still couldn't pull one on them because they would have enough questions to authenticate who you were.

After Officer Bogart finished filling out standard paperwork, he instructed the other two officers to unlock me and Tis and to bring us out into the reception area, where we were lined up side by side with the rest of the other inmates from the other buses.

After having those handcuffs and leg restraints on for so long, I felt like a man just set free from slavery. It took about a minute or two for my legs to adjust to standing again after being in that seat for hours. I had to pee bad as hell but didn't want to be the first person to say anything, and so I decided I would just hold it until I got inside before asking. The last thing I wanted to do was to stand out in the crowd.

My prayers were answered immediately when

a fat white officer who looked like Santa Claus came
out with a set of instructions that sounded like music
to my ears. "My name is Officer Harris," he said.
"Most inmates around here call me 'Big H.' Get to
know me and you will find that I can be a very nice
guy. But I am nobody's pushover by any stretch of
the imagination. I have seen and done it all, so leave
your two-bit scams at the door and we will be fine. I
will be processing all of you and that will take a few
hours. I want all of you to walk single file into my
holding pen. Take your belongings with you. There is
a sandwich bag and cup of tea for each man. Take
one and hold tight. I will get you downstairs and into
a bunk as soon as possible."

Wanting to pee had diminished my hunger;
besides, that tea probably was cold as hell and jail
sandwiches-well, let's just say the only thing on my
mind was taking a piss. We all walked single file into
the holding pen like we were told and niggers went
scrambling for the sandwich bags, as if they had
something different or special. I went straight for the
toilet. Good thing I didn't have to shit because it was
as filthy as an abandoned tenement building. There
was piss all over the toilet and damn-near a whole
roll of toilet paper floating in the toilet basin swim-
ming in an ocean of urine.

Close up, the stench was unbearable. I had to
hold my nose while peeing just to keep from going
into a coma from the intoxicating fumes. As the
bright yellow liquid passed through my urinary tract

I began to feel a sense of relief. When I turned around, I was surprised to see that there was nowhere for me to sit down. Like typical niggers, some decided to stretch out over the concrete slabs. I was not about to stand up for God knows how long.

To make matters worse, it was cold enough already in there and the floor was even colder. Was I supposed to sit on the floor like some Herb and catch a hernia? Hell no! This was my first moment of truth. Somebody was going to let me at least sit down. It's the little things, like how you respond to this situation that will make or break a nigger in the system. If I had to challenge someone for a seat, it wasn't going to be someone who was just sitting down. I had to go for the person who felt like he could lay down and hog the seat from me.

I surveyed the room and picked the one that I felt I could have a good chance at beating…if it went that far. In situations like this, no one is trying to go for the biggest and baddest nigger. I just wanted a seat, and if I could make a little name for myself in the process then it was a win-win situation.

There was an old-timer with his leg extended at the portion where both ends of the concrete slab joined. He was a perfect candidate because he was not too young and not too old, just right. He looked big enough to handle himself. I assumed he was an old timer by the way he just fit right into the process. He was comfortable because he had done this before. He also had a youthful appearance…as if prison had preserved him.

On the streets I had heard older people around my way speak of the "prison glow," that clear skin that radiated when the sun graced its presence upon it. If you were forty, prison made you look like thirty. (I assumed he was about that.) His beard was neatly shaven, and he didn't appear to have any flab.

"Main man," I said with an air of apprehension, "can you move your legs so I could sit down. I would feel like a real Herb if I had to sit on the floor while you lay here all stretched out."

"First off, young blood, my name ain't 'main man,'" he said. "I probably got more time in these joints than you are old. I'm almost fifty goddam years old and you want to call me main man! That's what's wrong with you young boys-you don't got no respect for your elders. All you had to do was say, 'Excuse me, I want to sit down.' You are not going to make it in here with that attitude." He moves his legs.

"Thank you," I said, sitting my black ass down.

At first blush his response could've been perceived as hostile. I sat down happy that my request was granted and mindful of what he had just said. Fifty? I thought. Shit! He had to have done damnnear twenty years in my book to have skin like that. I didn't see a wrinkle on him. If all the old-timers in here look like him then I am in big trouble.

I sat there making a mental note of what I had just learned from my two-minute experience. Two things: I was not good at judging a motherfucker's age; nor was I good at judging who I should step to. He was definitely not the one. He gave me the impression that he was not into that young boys' "beef shit" and that if he got into some shit he was going to kill somebody-straight up and down. My approach could have been less demanding, I thought, and I shouldn't have included the "Herb segment" in my oral presentation.

All of this was practice for what the fuck I needed to be prepared for upstairs. I was just relieved everything turned out okay. I knew I had to work on what I would do should a situation go to the next level. I had better have a solution for every situation at a moment's notice. He could have sensed in my delivery that I was just some young punk who didn't know any better. Hell, he also knew I was just a kid and this had to be my first time.

We sat there for hours in that holding pen with no word from anyone as to when we would be moving. No one seemed to be bucking about it either, not even Tislam. He was as quiet as a church mouse. Maybe Rico was on his mind.

Could it be everyone was facing their own demons and fears? Well, at least, that would have explained it for the first-timers; I figured old-timers had very little to say because they had walked this road before and to them it was just business as usual.

The concrete walls began to talk to me, telling all about the people they had come in contact with and the many things they had witnessed. The dried-up blood on the wall spoke of a fight that went far beyond a "talk beef." It spoke of an anger that expressed itself so violently the walls refused to give up the blood. In almost every nook and cranny of the walls were remnants of some foul individuals who sought to express their anger at the system by hawk spitting on the walls, and I had to take all of that shit in.

With every breath I anticipated the impact that those germs would have on my feeble heart, having been struck with a near-fatal blow of tuberculosis when I was twelve and spending several weeks in the hospital before they finally diagnosed me. I was coughing up blood and having sporadic seizure attacks. They finally were able to treat it by putting me on a drug called INH, which I had to take for well over a year. To date I have never been the same. It is oftentimes hard for me to breathe-when I am awake, I breathe as if I am asleep-and at times I suffer from mild heart palpitations.

Just about every square inch of the walls was covered with the remains of some soul who wanted to make his mark, so to speak, to leave an indelible impression on the hearts and minds of those coming after him.

Inmates had scribbled their names on the concrete canvas to remind us of their genius and the fact that they had passed through: Murder Mike, Bay Bay, Screw Face, and Don Juan were some of them. You could tell there was an effort to clean the walls, but the walls did not want to part with the "works of art." It was as if the walls and the tools used to etch these marks were one.

If I assumed correctly, Murder Mike must've had just as much time as I did, if not more. Not many men will get a "murder beef" and not have at least ten years to think about it. He either had a lot more time left, or he had written it a very long time ago and was on his way back to the world.

There was no way I was going to leave my name on the wall. To me that was just a sign that you would be back. No artist wants to leave his work without being able to grace his eyes upon it at least once after finishing it. How else would he know if it stood the test of time? Besides, my ticket had one-way on it. I had learned my lesson and I didn't need a second or third bid to tell me that prison wasn't for me. I was determined to remember everything I saw, smelled, and heard while in this state of involuntary servitude-that was all the therapy I needed to keep my memory soaked in enough bitterness to keep me a million miles away from this place once I was released.

I could hear keys jangling in the distance. After hours of just sitting there like a bump on a log, I just knew we were all going to get a bed at this point. I needed a shower, too.

"Get 'em up, men," Big H ordered. "I need all of you to line up outside this pen and strip down to the bare clothes that God gave you when you came out of your mamma's sweet morning glory." His disposition did nothing to persuade me that we were on our way to a comfortable bed. He banged on the door to wake everyone.

What in the fuck is going on? I never had to strip down in front of anybody in Sparford. We never stripped down. At worst, we would have our pockets searched or told to wear our pants backwards as a form of time-out.

It took me a minute to realize he was dead serious. I had to see others do it for it to sink into my little head. I began to strip down piece by piece with a look of puzzlement. First my sneakers, then my pants, my white T-shirt, and lastly my underwear. I was the last one to be fully naked. I felt so uncomfortable. I didn't want to look in either direction for fear that someone would think I was looking at their "johnson." For the life of me, I just couldn't figure out what the fuck was going on. Couldn't they find a better way to humiliate us?

But the humiliation didn't stop there. "Turn around and face the wall," Big H barked. Our bare asses were up for inspection. Maybe the officers had a thing for men. After all, they spend almost a third of their lives in a prison and another third thinking about the shit that goes on in one. Everyone was further instructed to cough and squat. Then we had to take both hands and pull both butt cheeks apart. They wanted to make sure that nobody brought anything into the joint that could hurt either the officers or each other.

Out of nowhere, two trustee inmates came out to the front of us carrying hoses attached to a vacuum-like barrel filled with a white, powdery substance. We were all told to make our way to the end of the hallway to the showers and leave our clothes right where they were. When we got to the shower room the water was already on. (There were about twenty sprinkler-like spouts.) It wasn't hard to figure out-they we were getting ready to spray us with whatever it was they had in those vacuum-like containers.

After we were all wet, they simply sprayed us with it: a lice-prevention agent. That shit made me itch like no other-it felt like rubbing alcohol mixed with poison ivy. Thank God, we were allowed to wash all of that shit off. The soap they had given us didn't help in relieving the itchy feeling either.

(The soap had lye in it and was made by Corcraft Industries, an industrial conglomerate dedicated to getting the maximum amount of cheap and free labor from the incarcerated. Producing everything from chairs and blackboards for the Board of Education to highway signs all across America, Corcraft acts as a go-between for other corporations to make billions of dollars from crime.)

After we dried off, we were sent back to the front of the holding pen to put on our clothes and gather our belongings. I was relieved-the pace was picking up. I couldn't wait to get into the population so that I could see what I was really made of. Shit! It was one thing for me to try to convince myself that I would be all right but quite another to convince the people that mattered most in this joint-the wolves. I would have my time to prove this soon enough because it looked like we were about to go somewhere.

The trustees came out with a hand truck full of bedrolls. I knew they weren't for us to sleep in the holding pen. Directly across from us was an officer setting up a photo identification station. He had blank ID card badges spread out all over the top of the desk.

All of a sudden, there seemed to be a sense of urgency to get us processed. Apparently they wanted us on the next shift's count before they went home, the count being the most important thing in the prison. If the count wasn't clear, it had to be resolved at all costs and-no one was going anywhere. It's funny how inmates are considered no more than property that had to be accounted for.

That fact was driven home by the ID processing officer. "A'ight," he said, "from right to left, I want you gentlemen to come up to the photo station to get your picture taken. When one person is finished I want the next man to step up in his place. Make sure you state your name loud and clear when you step up here. The number on your ID badge will be the most important number you will ever need while here with us in the Department of Corrections: it is your commitment number.

"The name your mamma gave you means nothing here. Everything you are and everything you will become while with us is contained in your commitment number."

He wasn't lying either. Michael Fraser was no doubt a common name, but there was only one Michael Fraser with the number 86A2678. The number wasn't created by happenstance either. It revealed everything about me: when I came in, my race, what I was charged with, and when I could reasonably expect to get out. My number meant I was committed in 1986, I was African-American, and I was the 2678th person committed that year.

After everyone was given a Department of Corrections number we were given our individual bedrolls and assigned cells and blocks. They took us in small sets to various housing blocks. I was assigned to C-block. There was no movement on the block when we reached upstairs. Not only was it nearing next shift, but it was lock-in time anyway. Most of the tier was fast asleep, and the few inmates who were up taunted me and the rest of the "newbies" as we entered.

The massive structure looked like a big castle. Unlike a fortress built for a king or queen, this structure was built to keep people in, not out. Built by the Hudson River, only the top portion of Sing Sing was exposed to the street level. Everything else was below ground, so when you went upstairs you were still beneath ground level.

On both sides of the cellblock were cells above and below. There was nothing to prevent a person from throwing somebody off the tier and breaking their neck. I was taken to a cell at the end of the block-away from the bubble, where the police could see nothing. If I got into some shit, I would be one dead nigger before the police even knew that something went off.

As I looked up and down the tier I realized this joint was wide open. I could see how a nigger could come in here with a one- to three-year bid and end up with life plus. If you wanted to roll up on a nigger it would be no problem. I wasn't optimistic about my chances of survival in the joint after seeing the landscape and was too damn tired to really take it all in.

I got room service to my new home-an eight by twelve cell. I was all too happy to get in so I could go to sleep. It had been a long day. I went in that cell, took off everything but my underwear and my sneakers, and tried my hardest to get some sleep.

This was one of the longest nights of my life. It was as if I was awaiting to be called to the electric chair to surrender my flesh to onlookers wanting nothing more than to see volts upon volts surge through my body until I was a lifeless corpse. I would wake up damn-near every half-hour through the night, mostly because I was scared to death and because I had to get up and pee a lot.

Before I took my last piss for the night I made sure to get on my knees and invoke the power of God to protect me in this chaotic place, to give me strength and courage. If there was ever a time that I felt I needed the blessings of God, it was now. I wanted to know that if I had to die under conditions like these then at least I had made my peace with God.

Fear was all I could feel. Too afraid to stay awake and too afraid to go to sleep, I decided I would relax my body to the point where it would rejuvenate itself without being oblivious to the things around me. No matter what, I had to deal with it.

CHAPTER FOUR

It was about six o'clock in the morning when I awoke to the opening of my cell door. I jumped up as fast as I could, prepared for the worst. All the lights on the tier were on and there was some movement, but not enough to suggest that everyone was up. I could hear cell doors closing hard against the steel of other concrete cages. All of the cell doors were open and the correctional staff was closing the cell doors of those who didn't want to go to breakfast. It appeared that all of the cell doors on the block opened at the same time to afford everyone the opportunity to go to breakfast.

The guard was slowly making his way down to my cell, and I could see other inmates fumbling to put their clothes on so that they could go to breakfast. Some had nothing on but their underwear, with the rest of their belongings in their hands so that they could get dressed on the tier because the guard was in the process of closing their cell doors on them. As he inched closer to my cell I made the decision that I was going to go to breakfast. I wasn't that hungry; I just wanted to get a feel for the jail while most of the inmates were still in their beds, figuring the less I looked out of place, the better my chances of survival. At least when everyone got up I would know how to get to the "chow hall."

By the time the officer had reached my cell, I barely had my pants on. I was going to jump out of the cell like everyone else. He didn't have any sympathy for the fact that I was new either-he tried to lock the cell door with me in it! (It was all too apparent who the newbies were-they all had state-issued green shirts and pants, the only thing setting them apart being their footwear.) I didn't want to stare, but I saw some of the flyest footwear in the joint. I saw shit that they didn't even have out on the street. How could this be? How could motherfuckers in jail be dressed better than niggers on the street? I mean there were sneakers and boots of all flavors and styles and some of the timepieces and jewelry niggers had on made Mr. T's gold look like kiddy jewelry. I could see why niggers always write to their homeboys in the street talking about they chilling. They were living better in jail than the people on the street working all day, everyday, for a measly check.

As my bid progressed I would later learn that most of these niggers in here were living off of that same measly check their poor relatives were making. Because of their bleeding hearts, these poor relatives were sending the little "two's and few's" they were making to their prison-confined sons, grandsons, cousins and other kinfolk. These niggers were ordering all types of shit out of jail-catalogs like Eastbay ...

and others that catered to the prison population. As fly as these Negroes were, I knew they were on to something.

As we walked to the chow hall, I couldn't help noticing that we were all walking on the same side of the wall. A guard with a big stick stood in front of the line. When he hit the wall one time with it, the line would come to a complete stop. When he hit the wall twice, the line would begin moving again. (This was so humiliating, treating human beings like cattle or some circus animals.) In front of the chow hall was a metal detector that we all had to go through. It was supposed to pick up the tiniest piece of metal. I would find out just how useless this piece of equipment was five minutes later. As I passed through it, a green light flashed above indicating that I was cleared to enter the mess hall.

In the middle of the mess hall there were about a hundred round tables that seated six men apiece. Waiting on line for food meant being a spectacle for the other inmates to examine you-the line was about two hundred feet from the back of the chow line to the actual serving counter and broke off into your meal specialty for the last five feet.

There was a Muslim line: the Halal line-they had to have meals that didn't have pork products in them or prepared in the same cooking pots; you had to be a card-carrying member for that one; a vegetarian line; and a kosher line. Jewish people didn't eat pork either, but they weren't treated with the same

degree of respect as the Muslims. The Muslims had
an air about them that was different from all of the
other members of the prison community. They ate
together, shit together, prayed together, and stuck up
for each other.

When I got up to the serving line, a tray was
shoved out from the other side. I couldn't see who
was serving, nor could the server see me-unless, of
course, he bent his head down to look. The serving
counter was fixed with a steel-like covering so that
servers couldn't do anything to a person's food if they
had a beef with them, nor give extras to friends.

The breakfast-chopped meat mixed with a por-
ridge-like substance poured over two slices of bread-
looked like vomit. It was apparent to the guard that I
was new-any man that looked at that meal with disgust couldn't be used to seeing it or eating it. He
quickly put me at ease, assuring me it wasn't poison.
"Don't worry, young man," he said, "you won't die. It
looks nasty, but it's quite good. I eat it all the time.
The other inmates call it 'shit on shingles.' ".

Right next to the meal counter was a big alu-
minum drum with a Kool-Aid-like concoction in it. I
was unable to get any because I had left the cup that
they gave me downstairs in my cell. I didn't know
that plastic cup was for me to use when I came to eat;
I thought it was for me to get water or something
when I was in the cell.

I had no idea where I was going to sit down
and eat my vittles. I didn't want to sit at the wrong

table-whatever that meant-and offend someone. I knew I had to act fast, though; I already looked like a fish out of water and didn't want to validate it more.

There was a table with a vacancy that had a group of Muslims seated around it. I figured this would be my best bet; after all, they are Muslims. If there was going to be anybody in the joint that could understand my dilemma it was going to be someone with religious convictions and a sense of morality. With some reservation and trepidation, I took the vacant seat.

No one said a word to me, at first-I looked down at my tray the whole time, as not to offend anyone thinking that I was looking them in the eye.

"Hey, kid," one of the Muslims addressed me, "you better get with somebody in here real quick. There is nothing that tickles some of these old-timers fancy more than a young stray with no support, walking around here like a chicken with his head cut off-my name is Mustafa Mohammed and I am the Imam for the Sunni Muslim community here at Sing Sing.

"Everything in this joint is run by the inmates that live here. You have to find yourself a group of people you can trust to have your back and that got some respect in here, or you're going to find yourself falling victim to some overpowering men in here that might want to make you one of their bitches. I have seen it happen all too many times. You can either take my advice or disregard it; it's entirely up to you."

I thought to myself, was he trying to bait me or was he on the up and up? Why was he so interested in seeing to it that I was all right? I had nothing to lose and so I figured I better take whatever help I could get. I made sure to ask in a hard aggressive tone as if I wasn't really scared and that I could handle myself if need be. "What do I have to do to make sure something like that doesn't happen?"

"You can start by telling me your name." The other guys at the table laughed. "My name is Michael. Michael Fraser."

"Fraser. That name sounds familiar." He looked at everyone at the table with an air of puzzlement. Do you have a relative that's locked up or something?" he asked.

My look gave it away-the moment I feared was upon. Did he do something to one of these guys and now I am about to pay for it with my life or perhaps he is in here and I will be forced to deal with him and confront everything about myself that I didn't like? I might as well admit who I am and what his relationship to me is before it goes to the next level. "My father is locked up, but I don't know him very well. He got locked up when I was two and a half. I've only seen him a couple of times on a visit. Beyond that, he is a stranger to me."

Mustafa gave me a look as if the world had opened up to him in a new way-a marvelous light shone upon his face, like a ray of ghetto sunshine through the cracks of a tenement building. "I know who you are. I should have known the moment I laid eyes on you. You look just like him." He looks at the other guys. "Do y'all know who this is? Abdullah, think Green Haven...79; the rest of y'all think A-block, 81."

Abdullah gets it quickly. "That's Joe Joe's boy!"

"Yeah, you got me." I am thinking, why did I have to look just like him?

It couldn't have been that bad because they weren't gunning for my throat yet.

My father went to prison back in the summer of '73 for killing the husband of his mistress. From what I hear he killed him because her husband found out and threatened to kill my father. Who wouldn't threaten to kill the nigger that was sleeping with his wife?

My father catches wind of it-through none other than his wife-bitches ain't shit!-and decides to beat him to the punch. If a bitch will put her own husband in harm's way then women are definitely not to be trusted. He didn't spare her dumb ass either. She was there when he was going to handle his business and he decided she had to go for two reasons: she was a witness, and she knew too much-she was the one who told him. If she kept her mouth shut she would have still been alive today.

They gave my father double life for that. I never understood what it meant to give a man "double life." Does that mean that he has to do a life sentence and if he dies and wakes up he has to do another life sentence?

* * *

'Joe Joe's boy' was all Mustafa needed to hear to feel right at home with giving me the welcome mat of genuine friendship. "I knew you was Joe's boy, but I just wasn't sure. I mean I didn't know right off the bat, but I knew when you sat down here you could be his twin. He would show me every picture he got of you from your mamma. You know, me and your daddy go way back in here; he is the only brother not on the path that I would go all out for.

By "not on the path" I assumed he meant a non-believer. I didn't know my father well, but from the way my mamma talked about him, he didn't believe in shit!

Just then the guards hit the table and motioned for all of us to get up and make our exit from the mess hall. I got up and started walking with them at their pace.

"What block you in, young man?" Mustafa asked.

"I'm in C-block."

"I am going to send a kite to one of my peoples over there and let them know to put you under their wing until we can see about getting you transferred to D-block. Don't worry about nothing; me and the brothers pretty much got the jail on lock. We practice peace, but we stick up for our own. Just be strong and don't let anyone disrespect you in anyway. When we have 'yard call,' come out and I'll rap with you a little more. As-Salaam-Alaikum."

"As-Salaam-Alaikum," I repeated, not knowing what it meant.

They headed back to their block, which was right next to mine. A sense of relief came over me as I made my way back to my cell. I had finally gotten the answer to my prayers; with these guys on my side I knew I was going to be all right. Judging from the way Mustafa came at me he seemed to be wielding some power around here. I guess I owed my father a debt of gratitude; this was the one time in my life I was happy to have him as a father.

* * *

Never saying anything positive about my father, my mother had done very little to pass on good sentiments towards him. As far as she was concerned he was always a no-good, cheating bastard who threw his family away for some bitch. My mother never cursed-unless she had his name on the tip of her tongue. Calling him every name you could imagine-motherfucker, bitch, lying-ass cheating whore-she was glad he was in prison.

For one, she didn't have to worry about him beating the shit out of her anymore, and secondly as payback for cheating on her and making her look like a fool. She despised the man with a passion. And that's why she hated me so much. Well...hate might be a little strong; let's just say, she resented me. I think every time she looked at me she saw him and she couldn't deal with. In turn, she would take that shit out on me.

In so many ways I can see how the sins of the father rubbed off on the son. (I guess my father was a convenient scapegoat.) I could easily argue that, growing up with a single mother on welfare, I was destined to fall victim to the wilds of street because of his absence.

It was still early when we got back from break-fast, and I felt much better and more relaxed, like things were going to be okay. If I could stick close to the Muslims while here then I was going to be fine-even if it meant becoming one. I was prepared to do whatever it took to make my transition as smooth as possible. Shit! I even took off my footwear. I was down with the Muslims now and had nothing to worry about. I was going to lay my ass down and catch some shuteye until daybreak.

I took off my clothes and jumped back into

that bed as if I had been there all of my life and was out like a light two minutes after my head hit that pillow.

CHAPTER FIVE

I was awaken by the sound of a billy club making that clacking sound as it moved from left to right between two cell bars. The blinding glare of the sunlight beaming in my face through the cell window, a big black officer stood in front of the cell with instructions for me to put my clothes to prepare to see an institutional guidance counselor and to go to "Property" to file my shit there and pick up my state-issued uniforms.

Having only a couple of hours sleep, I was still somewhat tired. I could tell it was still early because when I looked outside the dew was still very much present on the blades of the manicured grass.

The light from the window was unbearable, so I did what I did when I was back at Sparford: I simply took sheets of toilet paper and, with some wet toothpaste, pasted it to the window and held it in place until it dried. That damn-near reverted my cell to complete darkness again.

With toothpaste already in hand, I grabbed my toothbrush and began brushing my pearly whites. I prided myself on my teeth. I was a shiny, black nigger with beautiful porcelain-like teeth and gums red as sugar cane. After brushing my "jibbers," I used the toothpaste to wash my face. (I never washed my face with soap-that shit dried my skin out and gave me bumps.) With its high concentration of fluoride, I could feel the state-issued toothpaste going to work on my skin in minutes, opening up all the pores in my face for my last meal to exit.

My waves, glistening like ripples in an ocean, were trained so I didn't have to put on a du-rag to maintain them. I simply put some water and a little Dax grease in my hand and spread that shit evenly over my thick, shiny, jet-black hair-triple black if you ask me-with its beautiful texture. I know it had a lot to do with the fact that I was a Guyanese of East Indian and African ancestry-I never mentioned it though; in fact, I tried to be as American as possible.

* * *

My parents migrated here when I was a baby. She was from Georgetown; he was from a little village on the west coast called Berbice. My father's father was a Hindu named Theophilus Josephus Fraser. For the life of me, I wish I knew how he got a name like that. I would hear all of my friends-and everyone else for that matter-talk about how much Indian they had in their blood. I thought they were lying and just saying it to escape being anything other than black, so I kept a very low profile about my ethnic lineage. To me I was as black as anyone I knew, if not blacker. I knew "they" would hang me just as readily as any Negro born and raised here.

I had no problem being African; in fact, I embraced it and wanted others to embrace it, too. I made every effort to show pride in my black skin, big lips, and buckteeth.

* * *

I made sure not to look too put-together. I had to be ever so conscious of where I was at ... around a bunch of niggers. Even though I remembered what Mustafa said about "having shit on lock," I wasn't going to take any chances. A man that looked too pretty in jail was inviting disaster, evident from my stint at Sparford. You had to look good enough for people to know that you took care of yourself, but not so good that somebody would fall in love with your ass.

As I exited my cell to go to the guidance counselors, I checked myself in the mirror once more to make sure I had my game face on. I wanted to see what others would see as I walked down the tier. Satisfied, I walked out of my eight by twelve with the utmost confidence that I would be taken seriously.

As I made my way down the tier to the bubble,

where the unit officer was, I realized that the thick concrete walls in the cell were drowning out the sounds emanating from the block. It was as if I was walking down 125th Street or something. For a moment, I almost forgot I was in jail. Everything that you could possibly imagine was going on: guys were gambling with makeshift dice fashioned out of bread and dotted with colored pens; cigarettes were being bartered for goods and services. As I walked down the steps I could feel the eyes of other inmates follow my movements.

The bottom portion of the cellblock was worse than the top. When I got to the bottom of the steps I was greeted with a blast of marijuana smoke-just a few feet from the bubble-the fumes almost knocking my ass out. That put my mind in a coma-like state of disbelief. There was no mistaking the quality of the product, judging by the look of satisfaction and con-tentment on the faces of the inmates.

The walk to the bubble felt like the longest mile. I wasn't sure whether I was walking slow or my mind was telling me I was walking slow. The C.O. banged on the window to get my attention and told me to push the gate open so that I could come out of the cellblock.

Just then I began to think about a Bible story my mother used to read to us at home-Sodom and Gomorrah. When I looked back at the block as I walked down the corridor, I felt as if I was in that city and that it was just a matter of time before it would be destroyed; it was just that wide open.

There was no way I was going to be living in here and not get into some sort of shit. I figured, since I was no better than they were, I had better try to either go with the flow of things or be rolled over trying to be different from the rest of the inmates. There was no room for normalcy in here; you had to be crazy to keep your sanity in a joint as wide open as this.

I was now able to better understand how a man's life could pass him by in here. In here he's got the best of both worlds: he can get high out of his mind when he wants to-he didn't have to walk far to the weed or dope spot, and he damn sure didn't have to do it in the cold; and he could get three meals a day, and a one-room eight by twelve apartment. With all the comforts of his meager street existence available to him on the inside, there was no way a man was going to desire being back out on the street. After a while, he could lose sight of his freedom and adjust to being inside.

I was determined, however, not to fall into that trap. I was going to yearn for my freedom every day without fail.

When I got to the end of the corridor I could see other newbies who must have come from other blocks waiting on line in front of the counselor's office. I simply took my place in line and waited to be called.

As I moved up the line, I began to think about

the quick rush I just got from the contact high. I would be lying to myself if I didn't admit that it made me forget about being in jail-even if only for a split second. Maybe I could get high every now and then to escape some of the time. What was I thinking? Time was the one thing that I couldn't escape. Just that fast-I wasn't even there a full twenty-four hours-and I was contemplating using drugs.

When the other newbies had vanished from in front of the counselor's door, I knocked with a degree of restlessness to indicate I was ready instead of waiting for my cue from whoever was inside.

A voice pierced through the door. "Come in."

I entered and sat down in the only available seat directly in front of the counselor's desk. He was a big fat white man with hair on almost every part of his body. I could tell he was tall as hell because his feet stretched way out in front of the desk. His face scruffy as a Harlem stray dog, he looked like he hadn't shaved in months, and the odor that emanated from him confirmed my assumptions about his concern for hygiene-you would think an educated man would care about keeping himself clean.

His academic achievements were plastered all over the wall. He had a B.A. in art and a master's in sociology, along with a slew of awards. He could tell by my facial expression that I sensed something foul about him. He also had that knowing look on his face-I could tell it wasn't the first time he ever got that kind of reaction.

He wasted no time. "Mr. Fraser, you are here because every inmate is required to chart out a course of action as to how he would like to rehabilitate himself while incarcerated. I am here as a facilitator, to ensure that your goals are realistic, doable within the confines of the institution, and that you fulfill any court- or state-mandated programs for your charge.

"You have some serious numbers here-and a serious charge to match; you will definitely have to be placed in anger management.

"Have you used drugs before? Most violent offenders have a history of drug abuse."

"Drugs?" I looked at him like he was silly. "I'm too young to have a history for anything."

I knew what I was up against now: he wanted to explain my perceived problems in theories he had learned at school. It couldn't be I was just coveting someone else shit and in the process someone was harmed? It had to be some deep psychological shit.

He continued with his assessment. "You will also have to finish school or, at least, stay in a school program here until your eighteenth birthday-that's state mandated for all inmates under the age of eighteen. You can elect to have a job or take a trade in addition to that-your choice; but school can't be substituted.

"Are you interested in taking a trade?" He pushes a white piece of paper in front of me. "I have a list right here."

As my eyes combed the list-there was shit like

metal craftsman, wood shop, barber school, culinary services, and horticulture-I didn't even know what the fuck horticulture was ... or culinary services-I knew a couple of them that I could pass right over.

I hated doing hard work, so when I saw wood shop I thought that I would be slaving all day. So that was out. I liked the idea of being a barber. That way I could be around everyone since everybody had to get a haircut. That would give me an opportunity to get to know people better.

"I want to learn how to be a barber. How long do I have to go to school? And how much time do I have to learn how to be a barber? Will I be up all day?"

"What does it matter if you have to work all day or not?"-He gave me a look that could kill a horse-"I have to work all day, and so should you. Don't forget where you're at, young man. If you were at home doing the right thing all you would have to worry about is getting good grades and becoming something of yourself when you grow up. My kid can't go to school for free and learn a trade and it's my tax dollars that afford you this opportunity to do both. But in answer to your question-no, you will not have to go to school all day; in fact it is only for two hours a day in the morning. You can learn to cut hair in the afternoon for another two hours and the rest of the day is yours."

What a relief! The last thing I wanted was to have to work and go to school all day like a Hebrew mule. On the flipside, I could see his point about going to school. It was just the way he said it that made the difference in how I saw it-he made it sound as if I was getting a college education on his dime.

After about ten more minutes of his spiel, he gave me a wooden pass and told me to go to the property room to get some sets of prison "greens."

I couldn't remember where the property room was and didn't want to ask, but I had no choice. "I don't know how to get there; I just got in here last night. Remember?"

"Make a right when you get outside of this door and follow the green line until you get to the yellow line. When you get to the yellow line, follow that line until you get to a door that says 'Property Room.' " I followed his directions and made my way to the property room. The door was closed, so I just stood there for a few minutes before knocking.

With pass in hand, I calmly knocked on the door and waited for a response. I was wondering how long I would have to stay outside the door before someone came out or even noticed how long it took me to get there from the counselor's office. He didn't let anyone know I was leaving his office; he simply gave me a pass. If I had beef in here I could have been left for dead right in the hallway and no one would know it.

I knocked again, this time with the wooden pass I was given. The door suddenly came open with a ferocious swing. "You don't have to knock like there's a fire or something," the property officer barked. He escorted me inside and told me to take a seat. I gave him the pass the counselor gave me.

"What size do you wear?" he asked coolly, trying to put me at ease for just yelling at me just a minute ago.

"What size in what?"

"Never mind. You look like a thirty-two waistline and a medium shirt."

He went to the back of the room and returned with a selection of green pants and tops. He laid them on the counter and told me to try on a bottom and a top. I didn't see any changing room, so I assumed he wanted me to change right there in front of him.

After stripping down to my bare ass the night before, I didn't have any problem stripping down to my underwear to try on some pants. I grabbed a pair of the greens from the counter and slipped into them with a one-two motion. To my surprise, they were a perfect fit. It came as no surprise to the officer. I guess after doing that for so long you can pretty much make an educated guess.

Needing his stamp of approval to ensure that I was to keep them on, I displayed the outfit to him as if I was on a catwalk modeling for a denim jean company. He nodded with satisfaction and told me to take an additional three sets from off the counter. On a big paper bag that he had retrieved from under the counter, he wrote my name and I.D. number on it.

"Give me the clothes that you came in here

with so that I can log them into your property," he said. "When you are released you will get these clothes back and anything that they may have took from you last night that was considered contraband."

I quickly gathered them from off of the floor and handed them to him, thinking to myself as I did, Why in the world would I want those clothes back when I am released? I knew it would be a long time coming and I was sure I would be much bigger when I got out. Shit...I planned on hitting the weight pile like all the rest of the big niggers in the joint.

Wearing the greens helped me to blend in with everyone else. It made me feel like an old-timer in the joint. I knew niggers wouldn't look at me as hard as they did when I was in the mess hall this morning.

It didn't take a second for the officer to come down off of his friendly high. As soon as I had my stuff he was just as nasty as when he answered the door. "All right-you got your shit; this is not a hang-out-you got about ten good minutes to get back to your block. Take this pass with you and give this receipt to the block officer when you get back."

I better be ever so careful about trying to get cool with these correctional staff in here, I thought; they will flip on you quick.

I took the pass originally given to me by the counselor and grabbed the newly-issued greens. In addition to I had a pink slip indicating the items I had given him to be stored in property until my release. With all of that shit in my hand, my fingers struggled to find the doorknob. I had to put all of the items on the floor to open the door and pick them up again.

I walked out and began counting to myself faster than normal to make sure I got back to the block before my ten minutes was up. The last thing I needed was to piss off one of the guards my first full day in this motherfucker. I followed the lines back to my cellblock and got there within about five or so minutes. I had no intention of bullshitting; neither did I have anybody to bullshit with.

When I got to the gate, I saw almost the entire block running towards the gate. For a moment it looked like they were about to riot and take over the joint. Then I heard an announcement over the P.A. system. "Second call, blocks A through D. Yard call. Yard call!"

I remembered the Muslim brother, Mustafa, told me to come out when they called yard. I gave the C.O. my pass and the pink slip that the property officer gave me and told him I wanted to go to the yard.

"What's your cell number?" the C.O. asked.

"I don't know," I said. He looked it up for me.

Meanwhile everyone was still filing out to go to the yard. I was afraid I was going to miss the yard like I missed breakfast this morning.

He opened my cell door from the bubble and told me to drop my things inside, close the cell, and come back to the front gate. I ran upstairs to my cell as fast as humanly possible, my arms loaded. I didn't even bother throwing them on the bed; instead, I placed them on the inside of my cell door, right on the floor. I slammed the cell door and ran back downstairs at top speed.

When I got to the bubble there were still stragglers going out to the yard. I followed the crowd through the gate and down the corridor. Like sheep being led to a slaughter, the herd followed a long tunnel-like path towards the piercing daylight. When I got to the doorway of the yard, I was blinded by the brilliance of the sun's rays.

As my eyes adjusted to the light, I could see more and more of the landscape of the yard. The walls were as massive as the Roman Coliseum. On every side was a fortress of stone as tall as the eye could see.

We were like gladiators whose time had come to give the people a show to the death. An ocean of dead souls parading from concrete wall to concrete wall, blacks huddled with blacks, whites with whites, Asians with Asians, and so on. There were sub-divisions as well. Within the black cliques were separations by religious affiliation and gang association, each mob having their own brand.

It was apparent there was an unwritten code of ethics in the prison that no one violated. When one race was on the weight pile, the other races stayed off, and vice versa. Whites didn't mingle with blacks, nor did blacks mingle with whites.

It was the first time I witnessed whites not being scared of blacks; they were just as tough. Fewer in number, they seemed to be holding their ground. Some had tattoos reflecting their hate for the nigger-black people hanging from a rope-others had swastikas and Jewish crosses turned upside down.

At one end of the basketball court stood a group of Muslims assembled together like a football team around a quarterback about to give instructions for the next play. As I walked closer I could see Mustafa in the middle of the huddle. When I approached, the group formed a barricade until he summoned them to grant me permission to grace his presence. (That should have come as no surprise to me; after all, he did tell me in the mess hall that he had things on lock around here.)

When I got within arm's-length of him he embraced me as he did in the morning and greeted me with, "As-Salaam-Alaikum, my brother." This time I said nothing back; instead, I basked in his embrace. "Walk with me," he said. "I want to put you up on a few things around here that I think you should know about this place-the do's and don'ts ... you dig?" I nodded my head in approval, not knowing what to say.

We started walking around the yard, an army of Muslims moving with us. When we stopped, they stopped.

"You see those white boys over there. Those are the Aryan vanguard. Forget about what you see on television or on the streets about white boys being scared of the black man. Those white boys will kill you faster than you could spell your own name. And don't think for one minute that because they are out-numbered in here they won't fight to their last breath. They get by in here because of politics."

We continued to walk around the yard, and he continued to point out the various elements within the joint that I would be dealing with. "Those young gangbangers over there"-he pointed to a group of young blacks with bandanas hanging from their pockets-"they are a time bomb waiting to happen. They want to be dead and don't know how to ask someone to put them out of their misery. They are nothing but a bunch of thieves and cut-throats. I want you to stay away from them. Don't even deal with them-no borrowing, no talking, no nothing. Don't worry about them fucking with you either; they see you with the brothers, they won't try anything.

"That goes for those Spanish bastards over there too," he said, shifting his eyes to the clique of Spanish men a few feet away from the young blacks with the bandanas. "They can't be trusted; they will band together with whoever is in power at the time. I know they are cool on the street, but in here they only care about themselves. They are only half-black when it is convenient for them. When shit doesn't go their way in here, they try to band with the whites.

"I'm telling you all of this for a reason: If they're not Muslim, don't trust them. When you take a shower this evening, face everyone and make sure your ass is up against the wall. Never let anyone think you are inviting them to your money because they will try to purchase.

"I gave my white boy connect a couple of packs of Newport to get you moved today or tomorrow, so just be cool until then. Stick with me and the brothers and you will be all right-How you feel about becoming Muslim?"

There we go. I knew it was coming sooner or later. A nigger wasn't going to help a brother out for free. All he was doing was recruiting me for his own gang. I mean I didn't really see any difference between them and everyone else he told me to watch out for. But I couldn't say no; he would throw me to the wolves for sure. He had also made it plain that niggers won't respect a nigger trying to do it alone. I couldn't fuck with another clique now after they saw me fucking with him.

What the fuck did I get myself into? Fuck it! I thought. I went this far, I might as well do as the Romans do until I get out of here. "I don't mind becoming Muslim," I said. "But I don't know anything about it, though."

"Don't you worry about that. A Muslim is only one who submits his total will to Allah. All you have to do is make a profession of faith for starters."

"What's a 'profession of faith'?"

"That's when you openly, in front of all the brothers, bear witness that there is no God but Allah and that Mohammed is his prophet."

That's not so bad, I thought. Everything was

moving so fast for me. I hadn't been in the jail for more than twenty-four hours and I was already about to become a Muslim. That was going to bring me instant respect and credibility. More worried about what the niggers in the joint could do to my flesh than what God could do to both my flesh and my soul, the last thing on my mind was how it would affect my soul.

Just then I was startled by an alarm bell that sounded over the P.A. system. It was the signal for all inmates to go back to their respective housing areas.

Before we started to move toward the gate, Mustafa said, "There is a lot of things that you are going to see in here that may not be kosher to our religion. We ain't Christians-we believe in peace when possible and violence when necessary. On occasion, we may find it suitable to display a show of strength as a brotherhood.

"We also control most of the drugs in here: That's only so these savages don't abuse it and bring chaos and disharmony to this joint and none of us could live in peace.

"There is only one real forbidden zone in our brotherhood, and it will certainly mean your life if violated. No messing with these blade runners around here-we got a lot of them walking around these tiers; it's an abomination for man to lay down with man. That is a sin that we do not take lightly. You feel the urge ... beat your meat, but never let your carnal weaknesses overtake you in here, where you feel the need to commit to such acts. Do you get me on that?"

"I don't get down like that; that is not my bag anyway. You don't have to worry about me on that tip."

He patted me on the shoulder as we herded ourselves back to our blocks, satisfied with my response. I knew I was a part of the fold right then and there. All of the other Muslims hugged me as we departed and left me with the words that I first heard uttered by Mustafa, "As-Salaam-Alaikum."

I spit the words back out to the brothers as they uttered them to me. One of the senior brothers corrected me. "When you are greeted with the words 'As-Salaam-Alaikum,' you should respond with Wa alaikum Assalaam. It means peace be unto you, and unto you be peace."

Finally, I was able to know just what it was I was saying-instead of spitting back words that had no meaning to me.

As each brother hugged me I returned the proper salutation. I felt a sense of belonging and began to say it with authority. It was so much better saying it when I knew what it meant.

I walked back to my cellblock feeling like an untouchable; I was with-at least, in my opinion-the strongest group of guys in the joint. I knew I would have somebody behind me if I got into something, and to me that was the most important thing of all. No one was going to fuck with someone that they thought had someone behind them-especially if it was the Muslims.

The fact that they controlled the drugs in the joint was validation enough for me to know that I was with the right group of people. This was a world unto itself: "He who controls the drugs, controlled this world."

I was young but I wasn't stupid. I knew the power of drugs and its effects on people. I was a child during the crack era, so I was no stranger to how much control and damage drugs could inflict. But I saw my belonging to the Muslims as a way of keeping the other wolves off of me and, at the same time, giving me the respect that I needed to survive in this mad house.

CHAPTER SIX

Six years had passed and I was a devout Muslim, so to speak, and seasoned in the affairs and inner workings of the joint. I was as strong in the penal system as ever, the jail basically under my command. Mustafa was still Imam, but I was calling the shots for him. I had elevated myself during that six-year period as the go-to guy for Mustafa. (Some of the brothers were jealous, but there wasn't a damn thing they could do about it.)

By all accounts, I was even more powerful than Mustafa. I managed to do what he couldn't do: Bridge the gap between the Spanish, whites, and the young Bloods and Crips running around the joint. For me it was a simple thing to do. I had to let everyone know that it was in the best interest of all parties involved, that it was better to have peace than to wage war. I made it my business to take care of all the heads of the other factions through the drug revenue we were receiving.

My connections on the street were equally impressive-I kept in contact with every nigger that left the joint for the free world.

I had drugs of all kinds coming in from many

different sources so that there was never a drought. My Jamaican connection was bringing me up skunkweed that they were getting from a connect out of Miami. They would send girls up on the visit with it stuffed in the linen of their bras. The girls would simply go to the bathroom on the visit and leave it behind the toilet seat wrapped in tissue with feces on it, so nobody would touch it. When the visit was over, I would pay the sanitation crew three packs of cigarettes to retrieve the goods and bring it to my stash cell-where one of the chumps stayed.

My coke was coming from Broadway in Harlem. I had my man "Flaco" sending me pairs of sneakers in other people's names. He had a sneaker store on 145th Street and Broadway that he used as a front for his drug operation. He was from Colombia and well-connected.

I had saved his ass when he got into a beef with his own kind. The Latin Kings wanted him to get down with them so that they could control the drug flow in here by using him as their connect. He had a black girlfriend and knew how they felt about it, so he gave them the cold shoulder. That's when they tried to move on him.

I not only squashed the beef, but took him under my wing, making him my supplier. He had free reign to do as he pleased while he was up here and promised that when I got out he would put me in pole position, not to mention he was putting five hundred in my account every other month.

The sneaker operation was the best of all. He simply had the workers cut the bottom of the soles of the sneakers and stuffed ounces of cocaine in each sneaker. I had more coke in jail than some niggers had on the street. I would move the product in the mess hall through sugar bags. Since the coke was the same color of sugar, I made mess workers bring me bags of sugar. I would simply cut open the sugar bags with a fine razor, fill them with coke, and reseal them with a thin drip of plastic from a melted toothbrush.

I wasn't just a young nigger on the rise; I was that nigger. I just didn't want to go at the nigger that made life easy for me when I first came in. I didn't have to do shit in the joint except stay black and die. As long as I was getting the shit-I knew I was only as powerful as the last shipment-niggers were loving me.

My word was so strong I could get niggers to move on their own factions. A nigger would turn on me if I couldn't produce, so it was imperative that I stayed on top of my game. I knew that drugs was the only power base in jail, the only thing that can make a man escape the harsh reality that he may never see the street again. You take away a man's ability to escape all of the shit going on around him and chaos will ensue.

By now I had earned a high school diploma and a college degree. The state universities would come up to the prison and teach courses. It was a win-win situation for the universities. They were getting money from the federal government in the form of tuition assistance and federal Stafford loans to teach us. It was a big scam for them; they would get extra aid from the government for us as if we were living on their campus. Some schools on the verge of closing their doors were saved with this new infusion of cash.

It would have lasted for decades hadn't the local taxpayers caught wind of it. They pleaded with the government to stop the program because they felt like it sent the wrong message: that a motherfucker can catch a felony and get a college degree. I think they didn't want it because they felt like they had to pay for their kids to go to college while convicts were going for free.

All of my operations in the joint and on the streets put the brothers in a real good position in the joint and in other joints for that matter. I was securing a powerful base for us in other joints so that we could consolidate the power and instill the fear of God in anyone who fucked with us. If we had beef with you, you had to know that it would haunt you everywhere you went.

At the same time, I was slowly centralizing the power and focusing it on my ambitions. It was important for a nigger to know that the brothers weren't to be fucked with, but it was even more important to know that I was the brotherhood. I had to let niggers know that it would be virtually impossible to make a move on me because you never knew how many people had my back.

I increased the wealth and power of the brotherhood as well as my personal operations and power base. I was in control of the barbershop list, earning about eighty cents a day from the state and about twenty packs of cigarettes a day from inmates paying me to cut their hair. I also demanded ten packs a week from the other barbers that I got into the barbershop to work.

I used the bartered goods from my barbershop operation to buy pre-paid contracts from the Aryan Vanguard and the Latin Kings. If I needed a move made on a nigger it was paid for before he even violated.

If I gave a motherfucker some product on credit and he didn't pay in the specified time, I would send in the troops to do damage. The amount of damage depended on how well I knew him and his ability to pay the following week. The first violation would get him his right hand slammed between the cell doors-a tier one violation.

If that message was not clear enough for him and there was another lapse in payment, he would get a tier two beat down-a full-blown beat down with an option to have the jaw or a limb broken. There was no getting around it either. The only choice was what would be broken. '

If I was going to have a man killed in the joint-it became necessary when an old-school Blood entered the facility-I had to really believe someone was either trying to deliberately play me or the brotherhood. When there was unnecessary killing in the joint, niggers got uneasy and rallied around getting you, no matter how strong you were.

He felt like the Bloods weren't getting their just due and respect when it came to the way the brothers were running the institution. Somehow he managed to infect the minds of a few bottom-level soldiers. I heard through the grapevine-from an Aryan Vanguard, no less-that there was going to be a move made on the head of the Bloods and then on the brotherhood. I knew the information was true because I was their only supplier, and they had no reason to lie to me when the new jack had nothing to offer them. He didn't come with any connects or any strength other than himself, so they had nothing compelling them to follow his lead.

This was a problem that I knew had to be dealt with-swiftly. He was going to be made an example of and he didn't even know it. After I was finished with him there was going to be no way anybody was going to think about making a move on me or the brotherhood unless they had the U.S. Army on their side. This was also a move I was going to carry out myself; I didn't want anybody mistaking where it came from. This was out of the norm for me because normally I would just put a word of advice on a nigger and I would hear about it when it was said and done.

My weight was up. I was two hundred and ten pounds solid from working out for well over six years. I knew his little frail "buck sixty" frame couldn't stand up to mine toe to toe. It would be no contest knife to knife. I was going to display my cutlery skills on his ass and remind the masses that my knife game was still in play.

Aside for Mustafa being my ace "boon coon," I wanted the population to remember how I rose to number two in pole position. I mean I was Mustafa's go-to guy for several reasons: one, I was Joe Joes' boy and had adapted rather well on the inside; two, I would handle all of the brotherhood beef myself.

In the early stages of my bid I had no problem going knife to knife with a nigger. I just got tired of going to lockup. I knew that if niggers didn't see my gun go off every now and then they would think I was going soft. That is the saddest thing about having a name in prison and keeping it-you had to continue "putting in work."

My plan was simple: I was going to wait for him to get in the shower and catch him off guard. But then I decided that would not be a good way to show a sign of strength if I made a move on him when he was not adequately able to defend himself-niggers would never respect a sneak move the same way they would a move right out in the open.

I sent word to his cell that we were going to do it on Broadway, one on one, at the last recreation period after dinner chow. The "kite" came back confirmed and it was on from there. I had a few hours to get my shit together and to strap up properly.

I went back to my cell and began to put on my armor. It consisted of a bunch of old magazines stitched together with thick thread, and the hard covers of some old books. I placed them securely around my stomach and other vital areas to prevent a fatal wound to my torso. I was not concerned about my arms; besides, I didn't want to do anything to restrict my movement and endanger my life. I took a jar of Vaseline and smeared it all over my face and wrapped a towel around my face and held it together with thick strips of towel string to prevent getting cut with a razor blade. The Vaseline would allow the blade to slip right off my face, should the blade penetrate the towel.

My weapon of choice was a long strip of metal that I had fashioned into an ice pick with a handle wrapped with white adhesive tape. I put two razor blades in my mouth in the event I lost my ice pick and waited in the cell the whole time for my date with destiny. It had been a while since I last got busy, so my nerves were rattled.

When the cell door opened back up for last rec period I went straight for Broadway, the middle of the tier at the bottom level. The mood was set-the whole block was standing on the railing of the tier in a quiet hush, the calm before the storm. It was always like that when some shit was about to go down.

To my amazement, my opponent was no less

suited up, and in all honesty didn't seem the least bit afraid. He had a Rambo-like instrument, showing he meant business. We made eye contact and headed straight for the middle of the dance floor to get busy. He also had a small following with him. (I made sure to look at every face that was rolling with him so that I could give them hell when this shit was over.)

As we got closer to each other, the crowd began to close ranks on us to keep the C.O. in the bubble from seeing what was going on. We locked asses instantly. I pulled him close to me with an animal-like force so that neither of our arms could move anywhere. I began to knee him in the stomach, and he started biting me, his teeth locking on to my shoulder like a pit bull locks his jaws around its prey. I could barely feel it because of all the clothes I had on-two pairs of long johns, tops and bottoms.

I yanked away and made my move. When we broke apart, I grabbed him by one arm and poked him with my ice pick with the other, the downward motion penetrating his skin with butcher-like precision. When he saw the blood oozing down his arm he began to panic.

I closed in like a prizefighter, backing him up until he could go no further. I covered my face with both hands to avoid being cut and rushed him. Just then, he assumed a fetal position against the wall that allowed me to finish him off, each blow with my knife penetrating his flesh and bones. He was as weak as a wild boar in the wilderness being attacked by the king of the jungle.

His obvious forfeiture and weakness prompted me to spare his life. I slashed him in the face, carving the tick-tack-toe sign across his forehead with my razor blades-to remind any nigger attempting anything like that again that their efforts would be futile.

I managed to escape this one unscathed, but the niggers who rallied with him wouldn't get off so lightly-I instructed the brothers to round up every dissenter and mete out tier two punishments to all of them.

This was a critical and pivotal point in my relationship with the other factions in the joint. On many levels I had come out the winner. The population got a chance to witness my wrath and my mercy as well, not to mention the fact that I was still willing to get out in the trenches and put in work.

Mustafa was uncomfortable with the fact that I did it myself and didn't just send out one of the brothers. To him I was just trying to hog the light and secure control over the brotherhood, but that wasn't at all true. Someone had to be putting something in his head. I guess it could be argued that I was trying to usurp power from Mustafa; after all, I was the one getting all of the drugs in at that point, his connects having dried.

I wasn't eyeing the brotherhood but a bigger prize; they just didn't know it. Shit!-they needed me far more than I needed them. Besides, I knew they wasn't feeling me that much anyway. The only reason they were holding on to me as loyalist was because of the drugs and the control it bought. Without me there'd be no drugs, and without the drugs there would be a struggle for power that would bring about massive bloodshed.

I was just giving the appearance of being loyal to the niggers who originally had my back. I knew if I turned on them for reasons that weren't obvious then other factions would assume I would do the same to them and be skeptical about fucking with me: You can't get loyalty if a motherfucker feels you are going to turn on him like a chameleon.

I was going to have to capitalize on the move I just made right away if it was going to have a lasting effect. I had to make a decision as to what direction I was going to take next, concerning the operations and my jockeying for power.

If Mustafa was uptight with me, I had no time to try to figure out why. That could mean the difference between life and death. In prison, a move can be made on you from nowhere in a blink of an eye. I was either going to risk letting Mustafa continue to harbor some shit that I couldn't figure out, or I was going to take the better-safe-than-sorry approach.

A meeting scheduled to be held by the brotherhood at the next Jumah services further confirmed my suspicions. This had to be some bullshit because the brothers knew I had stopped going to Jumah services a long time ago, so to me it was obvious I was not meant to be in attendance.

To make matters worse I had to hear about it on the low. I couldn't imagine them feeling like they could move on me. Most of them were old-timers who were out of the loop in terms of how things were being run in the joint.

I stayed alert, ready to rally a bunch of confederates in a New York second. I was going to wait it out, though, not wanting to do something I would later regret. I made sure to reaffirm my alliances with everyone and assured them that the incident was by no means a reflection of any inconsistencies in my words concerning our agreements and my ability to be a man of my word. I didn't get any uneasy reaction from any of the faction leaders; in fact, I got complete acceptance. I knew I had all of them in my pocket to the point where I felt I could take a shower by myself and not worry about anybody making a move on me.

Ironically, I felt like if someone wanted to do the unthinkable, it would come from the people closest to me-the brothers. But I wasn't going to stress myself out over it though. Whatever was going to happen was going to happen whether I stressed myself out about it or not. And because of my "pity love" for Mustafa, I was going to wait until I got all of the facts.

CHAPTER SEVEN

After the incident, it was business as usual in the joint. No one even cared about it. I was bringing in the shit in ounces, pounds and grams faster than the product could turn itself over. I was also expanding operations by getting into new ventures.

My base of operations was the barbershop. I conducted all of my business there because I could pick and choose who would be down there at any given time because I was the senior barber, in charge of hiring other inmates to cut hair. I had been down there my whole bit. Even when I would go on lockup, I would always get my job back in the barbershop and managed to maintain my seniority because of a little payola. Guards-the smokers-smoked for free off of me.

Mustafa and the brotherhood had eased off of showing any tension towards me. I had to believe that it was less than genuine but in order to keep the peace I was going to go with the flow. I increased Mustafa's cut for the brotherhood to insure some level of loyalty to me because they were still eating … and eating well, I might add.

I was on top of my game, commanding the

respect of everyone within earshot of my voice. But I was slipping in a lot of ways as well … and didn't want to admit it.

* * *

Normally when I got out of the barbershop the whole jail was on lockdown for the last count. The guards were pretty trusting of me. They knew I wasn't going to fuck up the setup I had going in the jail, not to mention, they were all right with me. Instead of making me lock in and wait to take my shower after count, they allowed me to shower when they let Derrick out to shower. He was a homosexual on administrative segregation-inmates protected from the population whether or not they can handle general population. They thought that guys would fight over this nigger and cause a third world war in the joint.

He had taken female hormones while he was in the world that made him appear to have breasts and an ass on him that would make Jennifer Lopez's look whack. He was the kind of man that-if properly attired-could fool any man into believing that he was the genuine article. He also had long nails and some red lips that a man would give up his newborn baby for.

To tell you the sight of a homo repulsed me

would be a grave lie; in fact, this nigger would get my dick hard … and he knew it. There was something about the way the soap and water cascaded off of his caramel ass that tickled my fancy. Had he been an ugly homo, I might have felt like a fag was the most disgusting thing on earth, but this was no ugly fag.

Besides, I had never had sex before. Maybe my sexual desires were misdirected? On a subconscious level I knew it wasn't because of him that I was hard; I was yearning for a woman and he closely resembled one. I needed to justify it in my mind whatever way I could.

He would shower with the front of his body facing the wall as if to call me to action. He wanted me to see him as he caressed the crevices of his booty, cutting his eyes suggestively across the shower room right on my back. I could feel the heat emanating from his stare.

I knew he was feeling me from jump. He knew who I was, too-I don't care if you were on protective custody or not, you knew who was running things in the jail.

Everything I was ever taught about homosexuals as a Muslim was out the window. Shit, I wasn't a practicing Muslim any way. I couldn't remember the last time I went to a Jumah service unless I was going to meet up with somebody there to take care of business. I knew this was the one thing that could really force Mustafa's hand. This was a dangerous glass of wine I was thinking about drinking from, an intoxication that I had longed for from a woman but couldn't because of my circumstances.

Something about having a desire for him in the back of my mind was sickening, but in a sort of crazy way I didn't think it was all that bad, all things considered. I was desiring the touch of a woman, the scent of her lovely perfume, the gaze from her eyes, the warmth of her body. I wasn't a homo, nor did I love them. I was just a man who wanted the experience with a woman so bad, I wasn't willing to wait until I got out.

I had done a pretty good job at convincing myself that it was okay, but I knew it wasn't going to be okay for the masses. There were guys doing it, but none of them cared about what anyone thought of them because most of them were never going home anyway.

I had made up my mind that I was going to indulge my senses with a little enjoyment while cooped up, figuring if I did it on the down low there would be "no harm no foul."

All I wanted was a little head from the nigger; it was the other shit that had me bent out of shape-going up in another man or letting another man go up in you. To me that was really gay, but I could understand a man wanting to release a load into a nigger's mouth to rid himself of mounting frustrations.

I wanted to feel what it was like to have a set

of lips wrapped around my throttle, to feel the warmth of saliva sliding down my cock as I had heard men speak about in here concerning their women on the street. It wasn't enough to hear the stories, I wanted to experience it for myself. I was consumed with this thought every passing minute and the only thing that could quench my thirst was a drink from that well of sin. I needed a taste from Dee Dee's bitter waters and was going to do just about anything to get a sip. Who would know on the outside anyway?-unless you told it or someone found out.

The only thing I really feared was the homo telling. I didn't care that much about the brothers finding out because I knew who everyone would roll with should I need an army. I was more afraid of someone on the street finding out that I went up in some "bitch imposter."

His nickname alone-Dee Dee-sent chills down my spine. At first, I couldn't believe I was going out like that. The mere thought of what I was considering embarking on had my mind racing a mile a minute. There was no coming back from the shame of something like that. Distorted information in the wrong hands about a nigger's sexuality can be lethal for his career as a man.

Just what was the truth, I couldn't tell anymore. Was I a homo on the low begging for mercy from reality, or was I a victim of circumstances? I had no solid answers to my questions and trying to answer them only fueled further doubt. If I was going to commit such abominable acts I had to shed my garments of morality and purge myself in deception and lies.

That night I devised a plan that would afford me the opportunity to be alone with Dee Dee. Normally, I would send two barbers up to the protective custody block to cut the inmates' hair on the block. I didn't have a reason to go over-except when a nigger was trying to hide from paying a debt and figured that being there would save him until he was moved to another jail.

The next day I simply waited for the last hour of the day to call down their block, and I sent word to tell Dee Dee to come down. I knew he knew exactly what I wanted. He knew that if I was going to make a move on him for anything, I could have done it on numerous occasions when I had him in the shower. He didn't owe me anything and I damn sure wasn't into taking any ass-or head, for that matter-from a man. If he was going to give me some head it was going to be on his own free will and accord.

I regretted telling one of my barbers to give Dee Dee that personal message. (Even if a nigger didn't mean to expose certain things, just by the very nature of it being a secret could blow the whole thing.) Five of them came down, including Dee Dee. I assigned the other two barbers one head a piece and told them that I would take the first three people and they could take the last two back to the block after they finished.

I had seen Dee Dee walk in right behind the first man-that's why I agreed on the first three. When she came in I knew she knew the intent of my message from the way she was put together. My eyes saw an alluring, sensual woman, and nothing else. He had shiny Vaseline on his lips with a touch of Kool-Aid dust smeared gently over it, giving the appearance of a glossy-like lipstick on his already red, succulent lips. His eyebrows were also greased and neatly lined.

His greens fit perfectly around his ass and followed the contour of his whole body with the precision of a Swiss watch. He had managed somehow to tailor them so that as they reached his ankles from his thigh they would appear to be curvy. His nails were as long as any woman's, and his hair was slicked backed like an African queen.

I couldn't keep my eyes off him. As I signaled for the first guy to step into the chair, I had to contain myself from looking at Dee Dee, each look giving a little more away than I was willing to reveal in the presence of others. The seconds seemed like minutes and the minutes seemed like hours as I cut away at each inmate's head. Today was not the day to be getting anything special done to your hair because I had my mind set on a delicious plate of some bomb-ass head when I finished cutting and I needed to be finished as soon as possible.

The other two barbers had wrapped up their

assignment and, as I instructed, left behind them heading for the block. I was left with Dee Dee and the one guy in the chair. As soon as they all cleared the shop I retrieved three packs of cigarettes from my barber's draw and a hundred-dollar bill I had placed in a pack of Twizzlers.

The C.O. on duty was at the front desk outside of the shop was cool with me, I would hit him off on a regular, especially when he needed a few dollars to carry him over until pay day.

I took the cigarettes and pack of Twizzlers to the front and handed it to him. "I need about one good hour before the count today to make a few things happen," I told him. "I have to clean up a little in here and I didn't want anybody fucking with me during that time ... you know what I'm saying? Here's a little something for you and a little candy to hold you over until you get home for dinner. You feel me?"

He looked at me, then looked at the cigarettes and candy, where he could see the bill folded inside. "You got a half," he said. "That's the best I can do. I'll give you another half the next time."

Horny as a motherfucker, I nodded my head in agreement and went back inside the shop with Dee Dee. If he'd said five minutes I would have gone along with that.

"Dee Dee, you know why I asked you to come down here, right?" His eyes had given me permission to tread the waters of my inner desires, but it wasn't enough. I had to hear him say he wanted it just as bad as I wanted it.

He looked at me as if he was waiting for that question all of his natural life. "Yes, I know why you asked me down here; I'm not stupid. And if I didn't want it, I wouldn't have come. Nobody can force me to do nothing I don't want to do. I am not some scared-ass fag who is going to let somebody just violate me and not try to defend myself or do something back.

"The only reason I'm on protective custody is because the administration put me on it. I know who you are and I know you make things happen in here. I need you to make something happen in here for me and I need you to promise me that you will do it."

Promises-I thought to myself-I don't make those. I wanted to get it over with so I could quench this burning fire inside, already a three-alarm blaze. "What is it you want me to do?"

"There is a brother in here that made a move on a very dear friend of mine back in '84 just because he was a homo and I want him to know that this person had someone who cared about him very much and would doing anything to seek revenge. Can you handle that?"

Time was running out. I only had half an hour and he had used up ten minutes of it talking to me about some shit I didn't want to hear. At the same time, I knew I could grant his request because I was that nigger around here. "I'm not going to promise you shit," I said, "but I will give you my word I am going to look into it and see what I can do. If it doesn't conflict with me or my operations then I will do it; if it does, then I will have to find some other way to pay you. Fuck what you said about a nigger not taking anything from you-you know who I am and you know if I really want something around here there is nothing no one can do about it."

I gave him ten packs of cigarettes from my stash and told him, "All I want is some head; I'm not into that other gay shit."

He looked at me and began to get on his knees without pushing any further about the situation. As his head made its way down to my groin area I began to pull down my pants. He started to feel on the protrusion that came from the outer layer of my boxer underwear. (I had on a pair of boxers and briefs, to keep my joint from jangling and moving out of place.)

When I had gotten to the point where my erection was to its maximum potential, he pulled my penis out of its sanctuary and began to fondle it with his lips, the residue from the Vaseline and Kool-Aid on his lips accentuating the feeling of pleasure as his mouth began to go deeper and deeper over the outer garment of my love stick. His head moved up and down and around and around as he stabbed his mouth repeatedly with my penis.

It was just as good for him as it was for me. Every chance I got to look down at him I could see him touching on himself, stroking his own cock from the outside as he was servicing me.

Every thrust into his oral cavity brought a newfound pleasure of its own. I was intoxicated with the energy it produced inside of me. I felt like I was being lifted out of my body and some metaphysical experience had just taken me to a place where the rainbows met the sunshine and darkness was as illuminating as the morning day.

The pleasure became so consuming I had to control the strokes of his head by holding onto his hair. Saliva all around the sides of my dick and my pubic hairs I extended both legs over his head ready for climax ... with my pants still on. I pulled him into me and pounded his head into my stomach, uttering a sigh of relief as I exploded into his mouth, now full of my delightful indiscretions.

* * *

There was no way I was going to disappoint this bitch; after all, I wanted more of his worldly pleasures and I knew there was only one way to get it. I hated to admit it-nor could I really describe it-but I was in love. In love with how this man made me feel. I was in love with the act of having a good time with a piece of bomb-ass head.

If this was a test of my faith, I would have failed miserably. There was no denying I had flirted with the enemy and he had won.

As far as I was concerned he was under my complete protection and I was going to do everything within my power to make sure he was all right. To me he was a bitch, and as long as I was in jail that's all he was going to be to me.

But who was I? I was conflicted on what I should consider myself. Was I bi-sexual-Nah? I needed a label that would sit well with my conscience. Something I could live with.

The perfect term for me was tri-sexual-it didn't reveal anything about my sexual disposition-I was only a man that would try anything sexual. It wasn't even a label that had to sit well with anyone else because it wasn't like I was going to announce it to the world. I just needed to justify it in a way that would allow me to live a normal life within the confines of these walls and not torment my conscience-like that was possible.

* * *

"I know you are down with the brothers," said Dee Dee, "and I know you and Mustafa are as thick as thieves. Word gets around ... even on protective custody.

"It was Mustafa who ordered the hit on my friend, and I want some kind of justice. Mustafa has no more power in here than you allow him to have. And as far as the brothers … they are just your pawns and will move with the strength.

"If you like how you just felt, then this little thing we got going on can continue for the duration of my bid-I got about six more months. If not, you can forget about calling me back down here again. And I know you know by now I am not afraid of what you can do to me in here because I have made my peace with life and death a long time ago.

Was this motherfucker crazy or what? My response was swift. "Do you know what you're ask-ing of me? And what makes you think you could be comfortable asking me some shit like that. It was Mustafa who put me on in here. We have had our ups and downs, but moving on him is not an option after all he has done for me. You better check your-self!"

I grabbed him by the throat. "I don't ever want to hear shit like that come out of your mouth again unless you are ready to die-do you understand that?"

I must have been too loud. The guard came in to see if everything was all right-one second after I had unloosed my hand from Dee Dee's throat. I let him go without a response because I knew his throat got the message.

I took a seat in my barber chair. I was stunned and overwhelmed. Dee Dee managed to fuck up the high from my sexual escapade. I wanted to continue the unnatural love affair I had with Dee Dee, but I didn't want him running his mouth.

The thought of Mustafa finding out put my mind in a different mode. He was getting a little resentful of the moves I was making anyway. This could just be the one thing that could make him think he would need to pull off some type of coup attempt. He knew he had power because I was able to deliver the drugs. I wasn't sure if he would be willing to risk that over some petty shit like me getting my dick sucked by some blade runner.

I wasn't about to take that chance, though. If I didn't maintain my position until the end of my bid I would be like a fish out of water. No one liked a nigger that fell from grace.

My decision was as simple to me as ever. I knew what I had to do. I just had to find a way to convince the whole joint that what I was about to do was not only justifiable, but necessary. I also had to do it in a way that wouldn't expose my intent until I had the opportunity to strike.

It was a move that had to be made sooner or later anyway-before I outgrew my usefulness and they pushed me into a corner, like a nobody. In my eyes I was just beating them to the punch. Besides, as long as Abdullah was there I knew that there would always be a problem or some type of dissent because he was the root of all of the backbiting.

I sent a kite that night to Dee Dee letting her know that I was going to do what he asked me to do. In the back of my mind, I wasn't really doing it because he asked me to, I was doing it because it was something I had to do anyway.

I needed Dee Dee to expose it for me. He had helped me and didn't even know it. I wasn't going to tell him my reasoning either. If he was going to assume I was doing it for him, then all the better. I wanted him something fierce and this was the one thing I could do for him to keep the head coming.

The kite was to buy me some time. I was going to rebuke Dee Dee when it was all over for even thinking that he could ever come at me like that again. If I didn't, he would pull that shit all the time … maybe even on me again.

CHAPTER EIGHT

As time progressed I became increasingly reck-less with my dealings with Dee Dee ... and more paranoid about the possibility of being found out by Mustafa-before I got a chance to make a move on him.

Me and Dee Dee-going just a little bit further with every episode-were meeting up in the shower on a regular. It was the safest way for me because every-one else was on lockdown.

The heat of our prolonged lovemaking incited me to take risks that I wouldn't have taken if I was in my right frame of mind. On one such occasion, Dee Dee and I were in the shower role-playing and acting out our most intimate of fantasies. He stepped into the shower waiting for his knight in shining armor to rescue him from a violent attacker. I could see the muscles in his butt cheeks calling for the water droplets to fashion themselves around its curves. His scintillating beauty igniting a spark in me, I was ready for a test drive.

He had a scarf around his hair to prevent it from getting wet. For me, the scarf served as a reminder about just how sensual and womanly this man was. I didn't see a man in a head piece; I saw a beautiful woman in the shower protecting her long, triple-black hair from the damaging effects of harsh, mineral-filled water.

The soapsuds produced champagne-like bubbles that cascaded down the ridge of his spine and disappeared into the running water. I could see his skin softening up as he gently lathered his body in a swirling motion.

Once again he had managed to turn my world upside down-my cock broke free from its slumber. I moved closer to his side of the shower, my nine inches of predatory rage ready to take his lips.

He grabbed my cock and began to rub it against the slit of his ass, the warmth of his body giving me a dizzy rush. Even though all I wanted was some head, I went along with his yearning to embrace my cock with his melon-shaped ass, not wanting to risk upsetting him.

My blood came to a boil as the suds from his ass meshed with my penis. He pulled my body closer into his until our bodies were one. His back facing mine and my love stick pressed hard against his ass, I started to feel the urge to bust off, but I wanted this one to last a little longer, to savor every moment made available to us.

I could feel the hair follicles around his rectum touching the base of my cock, leaving me with a cool, mint sensation. Caught up in the rapture, I placed his hands gently on the walls and unashamedly interlocked mine with his. I humped his backside with an impact that sent his penis slamming into the wall with every thrust.

Without warning my body started to convulse, a way of alarming me of an overload, that I was ready to discharge. Then my proteins exploded out of my cannon onto his backside, leaving me weak in the knees for a millisecond. As my "jisim" danced onto the floor from off his back, I could see his satisfaction, knowing he had given a performance that rendered my body useless for a spell.

Although I was incapacitated I didn't want to stop there. I was ready for a second round, so I turned him around to face me. When his eyes met mine I could see he was starting to feel something, like I was. I was passionately in love with this man. A love that demanded respect. A love so crazy I had to pinch myself.

How could something so wrong feel so right? I wondered. I was fucked up over this, my heart taken hostage by Dee Dee's subtle charms.

There was a deafening silence in the shower for a moment. Suddenly, his tongue was in my mouth and he was French-kissing me. I was too shocked to do anything about it and even enjoyed every moment of it. The kiss reaffirmed my sickening feeling for this man. He was no longer a fag to me, but my down-low lover.

With my strong hands and big biceps, I grabbed him by both legs and picked his body up off the ground, his feet suspended in the air around my shoulder blades.

He grabbed my cock as if to say, "I know what you want, and I am going to help you do it," and placed it in his ass, the soapsuds enabling it to smoothly sail up his love canal.

This was the first time I had ever penetrated anyone. I was getting my cherry popped by a man. If a woman felt anything like what I was feeling, I couldn't wait to get out to get some, but for right now I was quite contented with this piece of ass.

We kissed and kissed as I stroked and stroked and pounded away at his ass. There was no end to my pleasure, and my mind was in a world where it did not matter if he was friend or foe, man or woman. I was happy to be happy and in love with being in love. I felt like my body was levitating from the ground and the air was my platform. His dick was stabbing me in my navel area as I held him suspend-ed like Superman. He was truly flying, I could see it in his eyes. He was being pleased and he couldn't hide it.

Sucking dick for him was all right, but his true calling was having that cock poke his rectum. And I was more than happy to oblige.

Without saying a word his eyes told me that he was just as wrapped up into me as I was into him. I had always considered myself a hard-ass nigger, but this motherfucker had broken me down.

My arms began to tire, so I let his feet back to

earth slowly. When his feet landed safely on the ground, I wasted no time. I turned him around and made him bend over. The animal in me wanted to just have good, raw sex with him. I wanted to end the session with a bang … give both of us something to think about.

I rammed my shaft down his cocoa chute until I was two knots above "depth nine." I was almost at the bottom of the ocean floor when I hit a debris field of biodegradable waste material, which prevented me from reaching my destination, the mounds of Hershey serving as a lubricant on my manhood. I was as happy as a faggot in boys' land. A faggot of a different kind.

Jab after jab I could feel the opening in my penis spread apart, motivating me to cum. But I didn't want to cum inside of him. I felt like my secret would be exposed if I did, as if I would get him pregnant and the whole world would know of my private indiscretions.

I pulled out of him slowly when I felt the creamy substance traveling down my ejaculatory tube. When I pulled out, he got down on all fours and took hold of my nightstick and placed it in his mouth.

He took all of my love juices unto himself, consuming every drop. He didn't flinch or move a muscle, his facial expression confirming he had tasted juices like mine before.

He rose to his feet and motioned slowly for me to kiss him on the lips. At first I was a bit apprehensive but then I got over it quickly. To me he was my girl and there was nothing I wouldn't do for mine.

As we kissed I felt an unfamiliar warmth in my mouth-my semen and his saliva. I was fucked up. This had gone in a direction I hadn't intended, and so it was time to bring this episode to an abrupt close. The sperm in my mouth awakened me to a sobering reality-I had crossed some very ungodly lines-and I knew it would be a long time before my mind adjusted to what I had just done.

We both got back under the shower to wash away our wrongdoings. I took special care to gargle my mouth out. When we were both done, we exchanged small talk.

I wanted him to move over to the block with me. That would mean paying off a couple of guards and getting him to sign a release form out of protective custody, releasing the prison from any liability, should anything happen to him "on population."

Then I had to take care of my biggest problem-Mustafa. If I was going to risk exposure of this magnitude I would have to get rid of Mustafa real fast and gain the support of the other factions.

CHAPTER NINE

I knew I was playing with fire by holding this thing off. I had been making my peace with everyone and informing the masses about my intent to strike the brotherhood. I told faction leaders on a need-to-know basis and I had the support I needed to proceed further. The fact that it didn't "get out" yet was proof-positive that the joint was flowing with whatever plans I had. I promised every faction leader I would divide up what I was giving Mustafa and the brotherhood with all of them and that it would continue like that on a monthly basis so long as I had their support and they kept their crews in check.

Dee Dee was begging me constantly to make the move-quick. I was getting kites from her every-day by my C.O. connect and was concerned that things were getting a little out of hand. To make matters worse, I was missing the shit out of that nigger and wanted to see him bad as a motherfucker. I had decided prior that it would be in our best interest if I didn't see him in the shower again until I had handled my business with Mustafa.

Today was the perfect day to make my move.
It was the first day of Ramadan and all of the
Muslims would be convening in the gym for morning, afternoon, and evening prayer. With nothing on
their stomachs-Ramadan forbids Muslims from eating
during sun up for a whole month-I knew they all
would be weak and would surely crumble to a massive army descending on them like a swarm of killer
bees.

I had instructed everyone to be in the gym for
the afternoon session of the Muslim call to prayer,
there being an open house policy concerning regular
inmates participating. Every year Mustafa petitioned
the warden to allow non-Muslims to participate
because he thought that was a way to bring new converts to the fold. Little did he know, that would be his
demise.

I was struggling inside with what I was about
to do, but it had to be done ... or my ass was grass. It
was going to be either him or me. It was equally
important that Abdullah get it, too. As Mustafa's right
hand man, he would have stopped at nothing to exact
revenge for the death of his beloved friend.

About two months prior to the move, the warden had brought in the movie Malcolm X at the
request, of course, of the Muslims. The type of move I
had in mind-I needed to make sure no one went
down for it-would be patterned after Malcolm's murder. I wanted it to look like a random riot, an "angry-
mob" situation of sorts. The gym was going to get real

noisy until Mustafa would be forced to quiet them down. At that moment I wanted niggers to strike, making Mustafa and Abdullah the primary targets. Everyone else would fall in place when they saw those two out of the picture-I was sure of that.

Not the least bit worried about failing, I had the upper hand and I knew it-Mustafa and the other brothers wouldn't dare bring a weapon with them while they were praying and fasting. Not only was it forbidden, it was taboo.

As the call to prayer came over the P.A. system, I could hear the masses rolling out for the gym area. I stepped out of my cell and saw Mustafa and Abdullah leading the procession of believers and non-believers walking in unison towards the gym.

I had more than enough soldiers from the Latin Kings and black gangs, so I didn't have to involve the Aryan Vanguard. Besides, it would have looked really suspicious if a bunch of white boys had shown up for Ramadan.

In all I was about two hundred and fifty deep. Mustafa and the brotherhood would be no match for the smackdown.

When I got to the gym everyone was posted up against the walls and scattered about. The brotherhood was in the center of the gym floor, calling everyone to kneel down so that Mustafa could lead the congregation and the rest of the participants in the Salat prayer.

The plan was for me to move on Mustafa during the distraction, and the rest of niggers would descend on the brotherhood as soon as Mustafa was hit.

But fate would not have it go exactly as planned. When Mustafa got on his knees to pray, someone yelled, "Get your fucking hands off of me, nigger. You don't know who the fuck you dealing with."

That was my cue. As I moved towards Mustafa, Abdullah got up from his knees to see who was causing the commotion. Without hesitation I pulled the makeshift knife from out of my shirt-I had to hit him first, or he surely would have prevented me from getting to Mustafa-and stabbed him in the neck before he could even get all the way.

All hell broke loose in the gym, blood gushing from Abdullah's neck. Even though I didn't get to Mustafa, everyone knew that was the cue to hit everything up with a Kufi on his head. Muslims were dropping to the floor like flies, damn-near every Kufi wearing nigger in the gym that day falling victim to the sting of a bitter blade.

Despite the ocean of niggers and all of the commotion, Mustafa was still within my sights. He got up quickly and tried to make his way to the door. It was the first time I had seen the look of fear on his face, the look of a man staring at his own death.

The two Latin Kings at the door pushed Mustafa back into the crowd towards me. He turned around, and I was staring him straight in the face, the

coldness in my eyes betraying the unspeakable hor-
rors about to descend on him.

Eyes fixed on me, he backed up onto a body
that was already on the floor and fell over it. As his
back hit the floor I plunged forward with the blade in
my right and a rag in my left. The blade found its
way to the center of his chest cavity. I could feel the
blade going into tissue and ripping out flesh in its
way out. I knew I had to be as accurate in my mission
as possible, so I kept stabbing him repeatedly in the
chest … until his lifeless body lay dead on the floor.

When I was satisfied his body would move no
more, I took the rag from my left hand and wiped my
hand and the weapon. I could hear the guards on the
outside of the door frantically trying to get in. They
couldn't see what was going on because there were
no windows in the gym, and the Latin Kings were
genius enough to barricade the door shut.

When they finally got the door open, everyone
with breath in his body was sprawled on the floor in
fetal position. (We all had a thorough knowledge of
what would happen if they caught anybody standing
when they got in there.)

The guards came in like storm troopers. When
I saw the gas masks I knew what was next-tear gas.
Everyone was gasping for air as they pulled us out of
there one by one in handcuffs. No one was spared a
beating with the nightsticks.

After all of the survivors were pulled out, nine
lifeless bodies were carted. I was still on the floor

when they brought out Mustafa's body, his eyes wide open in shock and disappointment. They spoke of a man that looked like he had been betrayed by his best friend or his son.

*   *   *

Mustafa didn't have any kids. Like me, he had come to prison at an early age. I was, in a lot of ways, the son he'd never had. Even though Abdullah was his sidekick, I was truly his friend; he could talk to me about things he just couldn't talk to Abdullah about.

When I began to think about what I had done, my soul began to weep. What I had done was truly unforgivable. My only comfort (?) was knowing that, in some ways, we were as far apart as the sun and earth ... with respect to my situation with Dee Dee. It had come down to self-preservation, and my life was certainly more important than his.

Dee Dee was a key ingredient to how I felt as well. I knew he would be happy, and happiness for him was happiness for me. I was going to get him moved with me the first chance I got, but not before I came back from lockup.

*   *   *

They had taken each and every swinging dick that was alive and well to the "bing." We could be down there indefinitely. Those who were fucked up badly went to the infirmary. I hated the bing because there was nothing to do but think all day, and I didn't want to do a lot of that. Not in my condition. Besides, thinking about Dee Dee down there would drive me crazy. It would only lead me to jerk myself off to death.

By putting everyone who was in the gym on lockdown, they thought someone was going to break down and confess. But I had chosen my niggers well- they all were "lifers," and so they knew the consequences of "ratting" on a nigger.

Better to be on lockup for the rest of your life than be labeled a snitch and be right back on population in this jail or another one. That would be suicide. (In prison you can't run away from a nigger. If he doesn't get you today, he'll get you tomorrow. If he can't get you in this jail, he'll have someone get you in the next.)

The moment I hit the lockup cell, I made it my business to send kites through every kitchen worker who brought food to the block.

Still, I was somewhat worried about the brothers telling. I had to let them know it wasn't about the brotherhood, but rather Mustafa, explaining that he and Abdullah were about to make a move on me for my drug connect on the street and that if they needed verification of that I would have my connect send confirmation ASAP.

I knew all of them would bite. They needed something to believe in, to justify not taking action against the situation. It was in their best interest anyway; they were weak without Mustafa, who was really nothing without me.

Everything was working out beautifully: The brotherhood was convinced. I was pretty confident that everyone would hold up to the fire, and it was just a matter of time before I was off lockup.

Every passing minute in that cell was torment for me. I wanted to get off as soon as possible because Dee Dee was scheduled to go home in a couple of months, and a few months with him just didn't seem like enough time.

As I lay on the bed, my eyes closed, I could see his oval-shaped ass, glazed in a shiny coat of baby oil … in a cell somewhere in the jail, legs wide open waiting for me to enter. His body was calling me and I could hear it loud and clear, like kindred spirits searching for each other while I was in limbo.

I jerked off regularly to his image, every episode putting me to sleep for hours. Then I would awaken to do it again-until I could feel the life being sucked right out of me.

My episodes became so intense they bordered perversion. I would take the cardboard tube that held the toilet paper and place my nimble dick inside. When my dick got hard, I would motion it in and out of the box, simulating the feeling of penetrating Dee Dee's ass. To intensify the feeling, I would grab my throat hard enough to prevent oxygen from reaching my brain. Just as I was about to reach a level of dizziness that would render me unconscious, I would stroke my cock until I came, the most intense and fulfilling nuts a man could bust by himself.

It got so crazy in that cell all alone without Dee Dee. I tried to pull my head down to my own dick to see if it would reach. Lord knows what I would have done if I got it all the way down there.

Each passing day fueled my perversion, and I was increasingly becoming my own worst enemy. I felt like I was losing myself. The heavy burden of jerking off so much took a toll on my balls, which started to sag and look disfigured. I had exhausted all of the semen from my testicles to the point that I was ejaculating blood. It was truly a sickening experience. I was in the cell counting seconds, minutes and hours.

Just as I began to feel like I couldn't go another minute in there, the cell door opened up. Two correctional staff came to take me to the deputy warden to hear my fate. I had one of them in my pocket-even though he was a hard ass, me and him managed to hit it off rather smoothly. He knew my position in jail; in fact, he didn't even have a beef with it. He would always say, "The only thing I care about is order in my jail." All he really wanted was for niggers to respect the game by keeping bullshit to a bare minimum.

When I got to the deputy warden's office, I knew things weren't as bad they could have been, given the situation-nine dead people. His disposition was like a cup of half-and-half coffee; I couldn't tell which way his mind was swinging. I don't think he really even gave a fuck about nine niggers dying-as long as it wasn't one of his officers. So where did that put me on his goodness scale?

He looked me straight in the face. "Look, nobody's talking. I don't know what went down in that gym, but all I know is nine people didn't make it when all was said and done. I've been fair with all of the movers and shakers in here, including you. All I ask is to be put in the know about what went down. Do you have anything for me?"

Was I hearing this correctly? Was he asking me to tell on myself? That was out. I looked at him with as straight a face as possible and said, "If I knew something I would definitely tell you; I know you're fair. I know just as little as you do about what happened. I was making my salat when all hell broke loose.

"I lost a dear friend and I haven't even been able to mourn properly because I'm stuck on lockdown. If I find out something I will be the first man in your office because that shit was fucked up."

He wasn't buying it and didn't even bother to outright reject my bullshit. His sentence was swift. "Mr. Fraser, you will have time to mourn-when you finish serving 1,500 days on lockup. Nine people have been killed and you, just like your counterparts who've come in my office for this thing, must give account for those nine men. If you don't want to talk you don't have to, but you'll get enough time to think about it. After you serve 120 days I'll bring you back before me. Maybe you'll be persuaded to talk then."

"Are you fucking crazy?" I spat, summoning all the mucus I could from my lungs and showering his face. "What the fuck did I do to get 1,500 days? I don't even know how much 1,500 days is. This is some bullshit!"

"That'll be 1,600 days ... and I can keep going forever."

Just then I was scooped out of the chair violently and taken back to lockup, where they threw me in like a rag doll.

The only thing I could think of was that it was a rap for me and Dee Dee. My heart began to bleed. I had to write her a letter. I started to collect my thoughts so that I could write something worthy of his reading and came up with:

Dear Dee Dee,

What's up? You know who this is. I am writing you this letter because I probably won't see you again. To even utter those words brings me to a state of sadness and confusion.

I have been thinking about you since the beginning of this madness. I just want you to know how much I care about you. You should know by now, I did what I did for you. Reading between the lines, I know you know what I mean.

I want you to know that the feelings I have for you is very real. It sounds strange for me to say, but that is the reason it makes all the more sense to me. I am loving you when everything within is telling me that it is insanity to love another man.

I can't bear the thought of thinking that I would never see you again. I hope we get a chance to meet up when I get out in the world. I don't know when I will hit the bricks, but I am leaving you my aunt's number so that you can check up on my situation from time to time. The number is 718-555-1212. Leave some contact information with her. Please don't let me down. I really need to see you at least one more time so that I can look in your eyes and tell you how I feel about you face to face.

You are my first in a lot of ways, and I can't dream of not being able to make love to you again. It really was love, despite what my carnal mind tells me. I am not going to bore you with a long, drawn-out letter. Until I see you again, love always.

MF

When I was done with the letter I looked it over a couple of times before giving it to the next "feed-up" person to give it directly to her. The letter, I thought, would relieve some of the grief I was feeling over losing Dee Dee. Needless to say, it didn't do any good; the pain was still there.

With pen in hand, I decided to convert the 1,600 days into numbers that would make more sense to me. Why did I do that? When the last number was carried over, added and subtracted, I realized I would be sitting on this cellblock for well over four years. I mean 1,600 days sounded like a lot to begin with, but when I got an exact number, it became all the more unbearable.

There's only been a couple of times in my life that I felt like I wanted to cry-this was one of them. I had already been denied at the board the first time I went up. And now going there from solitary confinement certainly wasn't going to help me.

Besides, how I was going to do four "joints" on lockup? The most I had ever done at one time was six months ... for a stabbing when I was in the third year of my bid. I knew it could be done because niggers did longer than that. I just didn't know if I could do it and maintain my sanity.

Confinement all alone has been known to turn a man's mind upside down. I knew niggers who did years on lockup and when they came back to population their screws weren't in tight. There was nothing left for the institution to do but either put them back on lockup or request to have them sent to a mental hospital because their brains were so fried up.

I was allowed two books on lockup: the religious book of my choice and a dictionary. I was not going to go off the deep end in there-that wasn't going to happen to me-even if I had to read those books to myself over and over again. What I did need, though, was some "shorties." I had a few pasted between the pages of my Bible, but I needed more, not to get bored looking at the same bitch.

If all else failed, I could just think about Dee Dee all day-my source of nourishment. I was as dependent on his presence in my life like the air I breathed. Dee Dee helped me to understand the realities of love and sex. He gave me great sex but that wasn't all. There was an emotional attachment, too.

Through a crack in the cell door I saw a white envelope at the bottom of the floor. Apparently it was slipped into my cell ... without so much as a "heads up." If it was contraband, I would have certainly gotten busted.

The letter was addressed to MF; it could only be from one person-Dee Dee. I could smell feces on the envelope but didn't see any. I opened the letter as if I was on death row and the letter was my last meal. It read:

Dear MF,

I received your letter and just thought I would respond as soon as possible. I heard through the grapevine, as you would say, that you got an asshole full of time on lockup. You were right in your assumption-I won't be here when you get off lockup. With that in mind, I guess I can be as honest with you as I want to be. I noticed in your letter you mentioned loving me. You were a damn good lay, but I am not in love with you. For me it was just business. I knew a little mean head and some "back shot" and I could have you eating out of my hands. It was easier than I thought.

If you think I didn't know you were just as bad as Mustafa when it came to homo-bashing, then you have lost your mind. I told you when I met you that I knew what was going on in the joint even though I was on P.C. I also told you I was afraid of nobody. I convinced you to make a move on your own man, and it was a bitch like me that made you lose your mind.

I told you Mustafa moved on a dear friend. What I didn't tell you was that friend was the man I loved. So, you see, I can never love you; my love is already spoken for.

I do want to thank you though for what you done for me. You afforded me the opportunity to have peace of mind knowing that the nigger that killed my man is dead and the nigger that did it was his best friend. You also have to come to grips with the fact that you are just as gay as I am, nigger! You might not admit that to anyone else, but you can't lie to yourself-you were in love with a homo. And it was this homo who not only turned you out, but gave you your first piece of ass.

You will always have a thing for some tight, bomb-ass, brown trout. I suggest you focus on getting you a nice piece of female ass when you get out. It would be a shame if you didn't. For what it's worth, you do have a big dick. Any woman will be happy to have a little of that.

As far as me worrying about you doing anything to me when you get out, I doubt I will even be around then. I only have 90 more days. You do the math and, as you would say, read between the lines. By the way, I am going to a halfway house in midtown for the rest of my bid.

As for me, I got other things to think about when I get out. You might want to burn this letter when you're done reading it. It is evidence of your crime, you know. May God have mercy on your soul.

Sincerely,
HIV

I couldn't believe what I was reading. Why was he doing this to me? At a time when I needed this bitch the most, she was shitting on me. I never felt so betrayed in my life. My mind just wouldn't allow me to believe this bitch was that smart, or could be that callous to set me up in some scheme.

The most important part of the letter was the signature. What the fuck did she mean by HIV? Was she serious or was she trying to scare me? And to think I went up in this bitch with no protection! If that was the case, there was nothing I could do about it now.

I refused to believe it; the lovemaking was just too real. Maybe he was protecting me from something or didn't want me to get my feelings hurt. I had to force myself to believe the latter ... for the sake of my sanity.

I would be lying to you if I told you I forgot about what was said in the letter overnight. In fact, I spent many a day in that cell thinking about its contents. It deepened my sadness and perpetuated my ignorance about what Dee Dee was trying to achieve.

I decided not to respond to the letter because I didn't want to further abuse myself. The best thing for me to do was to focus on the best-case scenario and just leave it at that: Dee Dee knew I was going to be down there thinking about him the whole time and decided that it was in my best interest if he soothed the pain by telling me that he didn't care about me ... so that my rage would make me forget about doing the time.

I was comforted by this thought and had thoroughly convinced myself of it to the point that I had forgotten about the contents of the letter and focused on the brave thing that Dee Dee had done for the sake of my sanity. And I was sticking to that one-whether or not that was the case-and it worked for me.

I carried that thought with me during the harsh winter months and hot summer days on lockdown. (The only thing good about being on lockdown was the fact that I now had an unlimited amount of time to workout, get my mind right.)

My regimen was the same, day in day out. I would get up for breakfast and begin to read the Bible from the time they woke me until daylight. Then I'd lay down when the sun came up until the next meal. After digesting my food, I would begin my workout: 500 push-ups, 500 sit-ups, 500 leg-raises, and 500 jumping jacks. (My body had become a piece of art to be studied. I was already a fine specimen, but my intense workout had cut me up like a chiseled Picasso, flawless.) I closed my day with about two hours of reading the dictionary.

I happened to keep my sanity; others weren't so fortunate ones. At night, I could hear the deafening screams of niggers who felt like the walls were closing in on them. Some would bang their heads against the steel door until they bled. The guards would simply take them out of the cell, place them in straight jackets, and throw them in the padded cells further down the tier. When they felt the inmates had had enough of that shit and were willing to be sane again, they removed the jacket and placed them right back in a regular lockup cell.

After two winters had passed on lockup, I kinda got used to it, becoming numb to everything around me, but still wanted to get the fuck out of there.

I was going up for parole for the fourth time-with a plan this time. I had done damn-near the whole bit anyway, so there wasn't much they could do to me, especially since my conditional release date was right around the corner. One way or the other I was going home. I just wanted it to be sooner rather than later.

CHAPTER TEN

The day had finally come for me. I was going up for parole again. I felt like everything was going to go well, all things considered. Even though I was on lockup, but I had still managed to accomplish a lot: a bachelor's degree via correspondence course from Liberty University. So I knew they couldn't tell me they were refusing me because of a lack of education. I had accumulated an arsenal of certificates over the years from going to one program or another.

When those doors opened for me to go see the hearing board, I began to catch butterflies. It reminded of when I was in the courtroom getting the time.

There was a panel of five in the room, two women and three men. I took my designated seat in front of the panel, in the center of the room. All of their faces seemed rather pleasant, but that could mean anything-I had seen pleasant faces before and was still here.

The first of the panel to speak was a white woman with curly hair. She was as white as the driven snow and her hair was as nappy as "Buckwheat's."

Her voice was low and docile like. "Mr. Fraser, you've been called down this morning to be heard for your suitability for parole at this time. The panel will ask you some questions which you must answer. You may not answer until the question is fully asked. Is that understood?"

"Yes, ma'am," I replied. "I understand." I didn't want them to think I was some dumb, ignorant nigger who couldn't speak properly, a sure way to get denied.

"I also request that you carry yourself in the best conduct during this hearing. Is that understood?"

"Yes, ma'am," I repeated. "I understand."

The second parole lady-she was a sister and I didn't know how to take her-took her turn on me. "Mr. Fraser," she said, "why should you be paroled, especially considering that you are on solitary right now?"

Why did she have to go there? It had to be the sister to ask a question like that. They'll deny you just because they don't want their colleagues to think it's a black thing.

I made sure to think about the question and my answer before opening my mouth. "I should be paroled," I said, "because I already have a life sentence knowing that innocent blood has been shed by my hands. I am totally reprehensible-from now until eternity. It will not make the pain of what I've done any less bearable if you kept me locked up for the remainder of my sentence, which is not long. I know that my actions were morally wrong. I can only hope I am afforded the opportunity to make amends by deterring others from falling into the same situation as I did. That is why I should be paroled.

"As you can see, my infractions are minimal, for the length of time I have been incarcerated. I think the records will reflect that. This incident I was given a solitary sentence for was a result of being at the wrong place at the wrong time-I was in the gym when it happened-merely trying to practice my faith when all hell broke loose."

The panel seemed impressed with my poise and delivery, but they weren't finished with me yet. One of the men on the board wanted his say as well. "All right, Mr. Fraser, I see your institutional record is impeccable, with the exception of this isolated incident, and a few at the early stages of your bid. Considering the violent nature of your crime, how did you manage to pull this off?"

"Sir, for well over ten years I have been paying a debt to society that I myself don't think I can ever repay because life was lost. I have come to understand that, if life can be taken by my hands due to my ignorance, the least I can do is deter others from making the same bad decisions that I've made.

"My only solution was to better myself through education, to better my situation and the situation of others. I earned a bachelor's of science in Business Administration from an accredited university."

The panel was stunned. I was a baby Malcolm X in there.

The white lady dismissed me, "Uh ... we have no further questions. That will be all. You are excused."

That will be all? I thought to myself. What about the rest of the questions?

I had been asked far more questions than that on previous parole hearings. I was pretty confident, but the swiftness of the hearing and the silence of the rest of the panel left me with an uneven, edgy feeling.

Naturally, I had assumed that I was being denied because the rest of them didn't say a word, and it was over so abruptly. They simply sent me back to my cell.

Several days later I would receive a letter from the parole board granting me full parole, meaning my release was unconditional-I didn't have to go to a halfway house or nothing.

I had used my aunt as my home plan; she was the only one sending me shit and writing me letters while I was in here. The last thing I wanted to do was go back to my mamma's house. Besides, I learned from one of the programs in here that if I wanted to change my situation I had to change my people, places, and things. Most of the niggers I knew growing up either moved on with their lives and were doing positive things, or they were in the joint just like me.

I wasn't really worried about what anybody

else was doing anyway; I was only concerned with what I was going to do. With my education I knew I could land a job somewhere. It was just a matter of hitting the bricks and applying myself.

My release date had Friday 13th on it. I wasn't superstitious or anything, but I still didn't like it. You would think any day would be a good day for release after being incarcerated for well over a decade. (I couldn't understand why they gave me a parole date when they could have just let me go as soon as they came up with their decision.)

I had so many things to do and so little time to do it. My date was only a week away. I was able to make ten-minute phone calls every morning up until the day I was going to be released. I informed my aunt that I needed some clothes and that I would give her the money when I hit the bricks if she could pick me up a few things. (I had well over $9,000 in my account from the moves that I was making in the joint when I was doing my thing.)

She agreed to do it-I was going to bless her with some chips the moment I hit her door. She sent me my clothes express mail, explaining that she couldn't take off to pick me up but that she would leave the key with the neighbor so that I could get in. Which was cool; after all, she was doing more than a little bit for me, and I was going to be staying in her house. That was already more than I could ask for; I couldn't expect her to take off too.

I didn't have a desire to call my mother or even

let her know I was coming home. I was sure my aunt would tell her anyway.

The last night before release was the worst for me. I thought about all the things I wanted to do when I got out. And what I didn't want to do-like hustle. I was good at it in here but had no intentions of making it my life's work. The last thing I needed was to land myself back up in here as a nigger starting from scratch-I had wronged too many niggers to be trying to establish myself all over again. I had discontinued my drug operations since my solitary sentence, so my power-base in general population was nil-unless, of course, I could get the shit again. But what did I really care? I wasn't coming back to this place.

I'd made up my mind to walk a straight line. It wasn't like I was afraid of jail. Jail was the least of my worries; I just wanted to get busy living, having spent almost the same amount of time in prison as I had spent outside. I was more than capable of getting a job. Shit! I was armed with a college education. The vast majority of people on the street didn't have that. That must've put me in the top thirty percent in America.

I couldn't help thinking about Dee Dee. It was the weirdest thing. Here I was about to get out of prison after serving over a decade-I could buy a piece of female ass in the morning if I wanted to-and I was thinking about some "she-man." To some degree, that was my comfort zone. It was much easier to think about Dee Dee than to think about a woman ... considering I'd never been with one.

I thought to myself, it would be nice to hold a woman in my arms and smell the fragrance of her sweet perfume. If I was in a rush for any old piece of ass I could call one of the bitches that came up to bring me my packages, but the sad thing about that was they all were ugly as hell and, to be quite frank, I would rather fuck Dee Dee than one of them.

Even though I had feelings for her ass, I wasn't about to go looking for some mo' when I hit the bricks either. That part of my life was over. Once I hit the bricks in the morning, I was going to leave that shit alone-no more "pillow-biters" for me. As a straight man coming home from prison trying to get his life back in order, that wasn't going to be in the equation.

I decided I was going to make myself go to sleep and wake up in the morning a free man. A new man.

CHAPTER ELEVEN

I woke up that morning to the sound of the cell door opening, the last time I would hear that sound again-unless, of course, I came back. The guard came to my door and told me I was on the roll out and to pack my shit. I didn't have much to pack, with the exception of a stack of mail I had received from my aunt and a few other people who had graced me with a word or two in written form. I also had a stack of prison photos from various events within the institution and some "yard" shots. I wrapped them up in a sheet off the bed and made a fifty-yard dash to the front of the tier. Not the least bit nostalgic, I walked down that tier without looking back or saying a word to anyone.

As I was ushered to the receiving room, I began to think back to the moment I stepped foot in this place. I was just a scared, little, young buck with no sense of direction and an asshole full of time to think about it. (It's amazing how time flies. I guess that was easy to say because I had done it already.)

On the counter of the receiving room desk was

a brown bag with my name on it. The officer on duty pushed the brown bag to the edge of the desk, signaling for me to retrieve it and open it up. It contained the clothes my aunt had sent up. They apparently took it out of the FedEx box and examined it. You would think they wouldn't worry about shit like that. I was leaving, so why should they care what I was leaving with?-as long as I got the fuck out of there.

My aunt sent me a pair of Reebok Classics and a pair of Tommy Hilfiger jeans with an XXL Hilfiger shirt to match-and a Guess watch. Talk about style. I was all too happy to put the clothes on and feel like a human being again.

The clothes fit perfectly. She had obviously sized me up from the recent pictures I sent her. I could tell I had that "just-came-home-from-jail" look, the kind of look that could get you a piece of pussy in a New York minute, not to mention my flawlessly sculpted body that I had crafted over the years.

The receiving guard handed me forty dollars in cash and a check for nine thousand seventy-eight dollars and thirty-three cents, the balance of my account. He instructed me that the forty dollars was for me to catch the bus or Metro-North to New York City's bus terminal on 42nd Street, or the Metro North to 125th Street.

I could have easily taken the train to get to the city sooner, but I wanted to take the bus, to see if the scenery was the same on the Deegan as when I took it well over ten years ago.

I had to wait for an escort to take me to the Ossining bus terminal and to be cleared off the count. That meant waiting for the 7 to 3 shift to come in, to take me to the town bus station. It was already 6:15, so I knew I didn't have much longer to wait.

I could see the sunlight from an open window up above. It looked different from any other day, as if the sun was waiting for me to be released to show its full luminance. I couldn't have been let go on a better day, I thought.

I was antsy to get my ass outside. Being on solitary all of that time, I needed to feel the freedom of open space. Out of the cell for about two hours, my body was still adjusting to pacing and walking beyond an eight by twelve cell and a tier that wasn't any longer than six project bathrooms lined up together.

A few minutes after the morning count, the transportation officers came down to "Receiving" to take me to the bus station. For the life of me, I couldn't understand why one of the officers had handcuffs in his hands.

He made me understand real quick. "I am going to have to put these on you," he stated, "because you are still the property of the State of New York. More importantly, you are not a free man until we get you on the bus.

"Over the years there've been a lot of complaints from Ossining residents about releasing you guys into the town to linger around. Some of the guys would go home in the greens, creating an eyesore for the residents, so they asked the mayor to ensure that you guys were released out of town."

I couldn't believe this shit-I was on my way to freedom-in cuffs. I had given them almost every drop of that fifteen, and they still wanted to reduce me to an animal. But I wasn't about to let that shit break my spirit or get me upset, so I went along with the program, extending my hand without so much as a peep. He responded to my gesture of good faith by not putting the cuffs on as tight as he could have. Actually, they were barely on; I could have easily slid them right off. Who would run away or try to escape from their own freedom? I was being set free into the wild and had no reason to break the chains of bondage when I could wait a few and be set free.

When the count was finally cleared I was led outside to the state van. There is nothing like the smell of freedom, I thought. It will make a grown man cry, and that's exactly what I was doing-crying my ass off.

The morning air had refreshed my soul and livened my spirit as the breeze of freedom splashed across my face. I stepped onto that van like a man with a mission and a plan, ready for the world.

As we passed one security gate after another, I began to think about an in-house jail saying: "If a man looks back at the prison walls as he is leaving, he is bound to return." It took every ounce of strength I had to not look back. I wanted to see that horrible place once again from the outside looking in. I was going to start life off by doing everything right and this was the first step-not looking back. There was more than enough ahead of me anyway.

The town of Ossining looked so archaic, the buildings in town reminiscent of the days of Benjamin Franklin and Thomas Jefferson. They even had a Town Hall. I had never heard of such a thing in the city, but then again, what did I know? I was a child when I left and didn't know much of anything.

It took about ten minutes to get to the bus station. When we got there the bus was preparing to board passengers-it would have killed me if I had to wait around for the bus in handcuffs. The guards took me behind the building to take off the handcuffs. They weren't helping any by doing that because all of the passengers could see that I was on the van. When I reappeared from behind the building, the passengers were staring from the bus window like they'd seen something so amazing. I got on the bus with my head up, knowing I more than likely would never see these people again.

The bus driver, a white man, looked "country," like he was born to either drive the bus or milk cows. "That'll be $ 17.50. You going to the city, ain't ya, boy?" he asked, confirming my suspicions.

I thought to myself, 'Ain't ya, boy?' Who the fuck talks like that? I didn't know if he was trying to insult me or if that was just the way he talked.

I gave him a twenty-dollar bill, and without

saying another word, he gave me my change and motioned for me to take a seat by pointing his thumb to the back.

The Greyhound, similar to the "Blue Bird" I had arrived here on, could easily seat about fifty but had only fifteen or so passengers. I was the only nigger on the bus. I guess the only time niggers got on at that station or came through those parts was either going to jail or coming from one.

As the bus approached the New York Thruway, I began to look out the window more intently. I wanted to see if the landmarks that I had remembered on my way up were still there. I saw more open space than anything. All of the trees had been cut down. I didn't see one landmark standing that was there when I first traveled north-there was no Loehman's, no Stella D'oro bread factory, no nothing-and the scenery wasn't nearly as fascinating now.

As we got closer to the city, the surroundings became more ghetto, every exit on the south-bound side betraying the bizarre living habits of the minority. And I was getting a bird's-eye view of the madness from the outside. There was graffiti everywhere-on the Simi mountain range, on the side of the highways, and on the traffic signs. There was even graffiti on the road.

I would often hear the white officers discuss the images of the blacks that they saw on television … as if blacks were animals in a cage. I could understand why they had so much contempt for the inmates on the inside: The only time they saw a black in the flesh-the worst the minority community had to offer-was in jail. It was like my eyes were opening to some new shit. Suddenly I began to understand myself better.

The only thing that had me going was crossing the 135th Street bridge into Manhattan. I could see my projects. I wanted to tell the bus driver to just let me off right there and I would make it the rest of the way. At any rate, he made a left on Fifth Avenue and made his way to the Port Authority on 42nd Street and Tenth Avenue. Forty-second Street was just the way I remembered it-except for the missing porn shops. I used to come down here as a kid to watch the 25¢ peep show. Back then, the place was overrun with porn shops.

I got off the bus at Gate 58 on the top level, from where I could see the Division of Parole building. I had to make a parole visit within twenty-four hours of my arrival anyway, so I figured I might as well get it over with, since I was down here already.

The three-story building with "Division of Parole" written in big capital letters above its doors, stood alone on the block of 41st Street and faced the terminal. It was obvious to all who passed the building what people were going in there for.

It was crowded as hell when I stepped inside, some niggers still wearing their greens. A security officer at the front desk took my name and paperwork and told me to have a seat until I was called. It seemed like everybody had a chip on their shoulders. I still felt like I was in jail mode. I had to break my grill at niggers to keep niggers from staring me in the face.

After waiting in the waiting area for over two hours I heard the parole officer yell, "Michael Fraser."

"Right here," I answered, in a low voice, letting him know he could have used the same tone to get my attention.

I followed him to a back office where there was a long row of cubicles lined up next to each other.

"Have a seat," he said.

I was judging no man or nothing, but I couldn't get over how unusually ugly he was, the kind of ugly where he knew he was ugly and knew everyone else knew it too. His only defense would most likely be to treat people like shit. He was a black man with big pink lips and some thick-ass bifocals, his face as rocky as Stone Mountain.

"Mr. Fraser," he said, "I am not here to be your buddy, your friend, or even an ear to listen to your problems. My only concern is that you adhere to the guidelines of your parole, which I will outline for you. Although you have little under three years left on parole, I am going to recommend a nighttime curfew of 9 p.m. because of the very nature of your crime.

"You also need to be gainfully employed within the next sixty days, or I will reassess your worthiness for parole and seek to terminate it, with the board's approval. Do you understand me?"

He had to be on some new and improved cocaine. How in the fuck can I do anything on a nine o'clock curfew? He acted like I was a pedophile or something. I was definitely going to display my disdain for the situation.

"Sir," I said, "no disrespect, but I think 9 p.m. is rather stiff, considering I've spent well over a decade in jail. My crime is the least likely to be repeated-the statistics support that.

"I also think it is a little premature to be talking about violating me if I don't have a job in sixty days. I don't know the job market out here, but I think I should be given more than sixty days to find a job. I am humbly asking you to reconsider both." I made sure to talk in a tone that allowed him to maintain his control and dominance over me-the last thing I wanted him to think was that I was some sort of subversive Negro who wanted to buck the system.

"Well put," he said, surprising me. "Not many people come in here and express themselves with the clarity that you did. I am going to bend, but not a lot. I am going to give you ninety days to find a job, and I'll extend your curfew to 11 p.m.

"If you have a check from the state, you can cash it at the bank on the corner. I will write you a note and put my seal on it. They honor institutional checks with no ID ... as long as we stamp your paperwork."

"Okay," I nodded.

"You need to come down every two weeks until I get to know you. Then we can talk about once a month. I make home visits periodically-I won't tell you when I am coming-I will come when you are supposed to be there. Good luck, and I'll see you next month."

He handed me the paperwork from the Division of Parole, with a stamp bearing his name and title.

I was glad I came straight off the bus. I could now go cash my check and have some paper for my aunt when I hit her door instead of waiting till the next day. I exited his office and was out the door, looking for the nearest bank-Chase Manhattan, the only bank on the block. It was packed. Everybody on line had a check in their hand.

When I got to the counter, a fine-ass black woman was there, to cash my check. She had a smile that could light up a room in three seconds. Her lips were red like candy cane, and her eyes were hazel. She definitely had contacts on; they accentuated her beauty.

She took the check. "Would you like small bills or big bills, sir?" she asked, stunned and trying to hide it-the check said Sing Sing Correctional Facility.

"I'll take it anyway you give it to me, sweetie," I said, licking my lips.

She laughed and proceeded to count and double-count. When she was done counting, she pulled a receipt from the machine and wrote something on it before handing me my cash. I could see she was feeling me, but I was too shy to ask her name. I simply took the cash, the receipt, and walked out the door. When I got outside, I looked at the receipt. On the back of it was her name and phone number: Diane 212-368-6899. I had scored-without even trying. Must've been that jail glow, I thought

I had a pocketful of cash and just about nothing to spend it on. There were clothing stores all over the block...like they designed it that way. I needed to get some clothes anyway. The only thing I had was what I had on.

I first went into this men's suit store-I was going to need a suit or two if I was going to look for employment. I picked out three suits and told the haberdasher, "I would come back for them in a few."

Directly across the street from them was Jimmy Jazz urban apparel store carrying everything from Guess to Karl Kani. I went nigger-crazy in there. I got seven pairs of jeans and seven shirts. For footwear, I kept it real simple-another pair of Reebok Classics and four pairs of Timberlands-they go with just about anything urban-and two packs of the basic Fruit of the Loom.

I walked out of that store with all of that shit for less than $1,500 dollars and still had over $7,500 in my pocket to rock with. I wasn't stressed at all.

Well over two hours had gone by. I was sure they had finished tailoring the suits for me. I went back across the street and lo and behold, they were in a plastic suit-bag, ready to go.

I had every bit of eight bags when I finished shopping. There was no way I was going to take the train all the way uptown with all of those bags. I sat the bags down on the side of the curb in front of the suit shop to wave a cab.

It took me about twenty minutes to snap into reality, to realize why no cabs would stop for me-I was a black man in midtown trying to catch a cab. I had to get a white lady to hail one for me and show the cab driver cash before he even considered taking me. He didn't even bother to help me with all my bags. I had to stuff them in the back with me. I was cramped all the way.

To add insult to injury, instead of getting on the Westside Highway, which was a few blocks over, he went eastbound up 57th Street, towards Central Park entrance. Now he could charge me extra since it took much longer going through the park and crossing all the way over on the other side of town. By the time we got uptown to my aunt's house, on 111th Street between Fifth and Lennox, the meter was saying $31.00. If I was broke at the time I would have pitched a bitch, but I had a pocketful, so I wasn't sweating it.

My aunt lived in the Florien West Apartments. The building was so different from how I remembered it. Apparently it had a facelift. The awning read, "New West Apartments." I was surprised to see an intercom as well. My aunt kept an immaculate apartment, but the outside of her building never looked this nice. She lived in 5C, but I had to press 5B to get in; she had left the key with her neighbor for me to get in.

A voice came over the intercom. "Who is it?" a little boy asked.

Why wasn't he in school? "Hello, this is Michael. Is Mommy home?"

"Hello, who is it?" A woman asked this time, trying to sound really professional-as if she wasn't living in the ghetto.

"This is Michael. My aunt said she left a key for me with you." She buzzed me in, and I proceeded to her apartment. When I got out of the elevator she was standing right in front of it.

She was my aunt's age, I could tell just by her disposition. The only difference was she had a body that was out of this world. Her nightgown revealed every nook and cranny of curves on her body. Her booty was humped over her back like two halves of watermelons strapped on her thighs. Her breasts were as perky as cassava melons. She was trying to hug me, but when she saw I was not putting the bags down, she French-kissed me.

My aunt's apartment door was wide open. The neighbor apparently took it upon herself to do me the honors.

I walked in. I could see the presence of my aunt all around the apartment.

(She was very Afro-centric; in fact, all of the cards and letters she sent me in prison showed that. There would be cards of the kings and queens of Egypt and other African nations.)

Her house was full of African oil paintings, candles and incense. There were pictures on the wall of her and my little cousin in African garb.

I heard footsteps directly behind me, walking as I walked. When I turned around, it was the neighbor. She had come in right behind me. It didn't take a rocket scientist to know what she wanted.

I placed the bags on the foot of the couch and took of my shirt off to unwind, to show her my body without being too obvious. Her seductive eyes were telling me that she wanted me bad. I couldn't believe it-I didn't have to look for no ass; ass was coming to me. That jail glow, I thought.

For a moment, I almost forgot I was a virgin ... in a sense. I wasn't about to tell her.

She didn't waste time telling me what she wanted either. "You are so fine, you know that."

I started to blush like a little boy.

"I want a piece of that," she said, "before these young girls around here get to you. You don't have to worry about anything; I'll be as discreet as you want to be-we don't even have to tell your aunt. You can have in-house pussy right next door whenever you want it, and you can still do your thing. I know you just got out and you are going to run the streets like a bat out of hell. I just want to have some fun with you."

She came closer to me and started to feel over my chest.

My temperature began to rise to levels that made me want to explode. I had not jerked off in a minute, so I was backed up with cum. My nuts were as big and tight as a baby's asshole.

I could see the method to her madness. She didn't mistakenly come out with her robe on; she wanted to have easy access to pull off her clothes. This was the perfect opportunity to sharpen my love-making skills ... with someone I didn't plan on being with forever or making my girl. If I ever got a chance to go up into the girl I met today at the bank, I was going to be ready.

As she continued to touch me, I pulled the knot loose from the robe and watched it fall to the floor.

(My aunt worked until six everyday. I knew that because she told me, when I was in jail, "never call before 6:30 because I get off at six and I need a half an hour to get home." It was only four o' clock; I had ample time.)

Her body looked better than I could ever have imagined. The robe did her body a disservice. I mean her body was banging with the robe on, but with the robe off she looked like she could be a playboy cen-terfold. If she wasn't my aunt's age, I would "wife" her.

I wanted to get real freaky with her. I told her,

"I bet I can flip you and fuck you before you can throw me and blow me." That fucked her head up; it took her a second to catch it.

Her pussy was as pretty as a Hollywood Uterus. Her tits stood at attention, defying gravity. I saluted them by sucking gently on each nipple. I wasn't a total novice, I pretty much knew what I was doing-from reading porn magazines and fucking Dee Dee.

She placed her arms around my neck, and we started to slob each other in the mouth, exchanging spit without conscience. I pushed her on the couch and went downtown. I pulled the bulb of her clitoris back so that it could protrude far enough for me to lick on it without the foreskin getting in the way. As I massaged the clitoris with my tongue, her moans became erratic and intense.

She grabbed onto my bare skin and started to dig her nails deep into my shoulder. When she could take no more, I pulled my tongue out of her garage so I could park my penis inside.

I stood up off the floor and lifted her legs up as if changing a baby's diaper. Slowly inserting my hustler's cock into her wet mound, I began to drill her with brute force. She started screaming. She told me, "Keep fucking me like that … it hurt so good."

I was a pro and didn't even know it. All I was really doing was thinking about how I was fucking the shit out of Dee Dee. Dee Dee, being a man, was much heavier and thick-skinned than she was, so it was easier for me to manipulate her.

I grabbed a napkin ring from my aunt's table-it looked like it could fit my cock-and slipped it on my dick to prevent it from becoming flaccid. It snapped right back to action as soon as the ring touched the base of my pelvic bone. I started to pound her guts like I was harpooning a whale. I was going so deep inside of her I could feel the tip of my rod hitting up against the lining of her stomach.

When I was ready to explode, I simply withdrew my gun and gave her a "pearl necklace." She took her right hand and started smearing it on her skin like lotion. As the white paste began to dry around her neck, she took my dick in hand and began to rob me of the rest of my bodily fluids. She sucked me bone dry.

My first experience had been a success-and I didn't even have to tell her I was a new jack.

She got up off the floor and put her robe back on happy as a catholic priest with a roomful of choir-boys.

Next door I could hear her son crying up a storm. He was probably crying all the while I was fucking the shit of his mom. I just didn't hear it; I was busy doing me-and her, too.

She made a dash for the door to attend to her little one's cries. I was happy for the piece of ass of course, but I thought it was a little careless of her. That motherfucker could have burnt his hand on the stove or took a bottle full of aspirins and she was over here with me boning me out with reckless abandon. I also knew that if she would fuck me just like that, God knows how many other niggers she done gave the pussy to. I didn't even remember the bitch ever telling me her name.

As crazy as it may sound, she got more out of the sex than I did. The pussy was good as a motherfucker, don't get me wrong, but in some depraved way, I wanted something much tighter. I was used to a smaller hole that could grab a hold of my dick like a vise grip. I was afraid to entertain the thought that a man's asshole was far more pleasurable than some wet, juicy piece of pussy.

Granted, I was able to do more with her than I could with a man, like eat her out, but the pros and cons of having some tight-ass asshole was worth pondering for a moment or two. I was conflicted about who I was as a man, and it was killing me. It seemed like I was no different from those I accused of pillow-biting. I mean I could easily say, "I never took it in the ass, and all I ever did was pitch." But the streets wouldn't accept that, and most niggers in jail won't accept it either. If I had to be honest, I think I preferred a little shit on my dick.

I needed to take a shower before my aunt got in-I still had home girl's juices all over me. The last thing I wanted was for her to think I was disrespecting her household by fucking in it.

With dick dangling and remnants of piss dripping on the floor, I walked to the closet by the door to get me a clean towel. I knew everything would be in the same place.

While in the shower I couldn't help thinking about Dee Dee. I was drawn to him like some cosmic force of nature. When the soap touched my "sweet William," I started to think about the times we spent together. About the time she swallowed my sword-"boy scout" style. She would hum a tune on my flute like Kenny G. Oftentimes she would lick my cranberries until face cream oozed out.

It seemed like my mind was more in a frenzy over thinking about episodes with Dee Dee than the one I had just minutes ago. I was able to bust off another round while in the shower. I stood there for an additional five minutes washing away all of that baggage from prison.

I got out, oiled up, and put on a pair of fresh underclothes and some outer garments. I knew my aunt and cousin would be home shortly.

CHAPTER TWELVE

Exhausted from busting so many nuts I couldn't find it in myself to go to sleep. It was as if I felt I was going to miss something if I fell asleep. I wasn't about to stay in the house on my first day out either.

There was nothing in the house for me to do. I pranced around from one room to the other trying to kill time until my aunt came home.

I was as free as a bird and still felt like a prisoner. I didn't have anywhere to go because I didn't know where to go. I could go to my old 'hood, around my mother's way, but I really didn't want to roam around up there, not knowing what niggers were up to or into. For all I knew, I could be standing around with one of those lame-ass niggers and get bagged on a "humble" for just standing outside with a nigger.

I had a homemade telephone book full of numbers, but those numbers were of niggers that I either knew from jail that went home, or connects, niggers I met while in jail through a third party.

Staying inside was killing me though. I just

had to get out. I had the key anyway. I'm sure my aunt would understand me going outside to get a little fresh air. I grabbed the keys and made a beeline for the door, stopping at my aunt's neighbor to tell her what I was doing so my aunt would know.

I knocked on the door. I could hear a man's voice. I knew he wasn't there before because I remember the little boy crying for her when I was digging in her guts. I banged on the door. The door swung open so forcefully I had to flinch.

Some chubby, "gump-looking" nigger-he resembled the little boy a bit-addressed me with a bitch-like, "Hello, can I help you?"

I responded like a man who had just come home from a hellhole with niggers far more dangerous than he could ever imagine. "Yea, you might be able to help me, duke. My aunt left the key for me to get in with the lady that lives here; I just came and got it from her earlier. I need to leave a message with her because I am about to run out for a minute. Go get her for me."

That was a "son move." I knew if he didn't check me on that, then he was a sucker. You don't let no grown-ass man tell you to "go get" anybody.

He didn't check me; in fact, he went to go get her as if he was my son or something. He could never get any respect from me from here on out. I took it upon myself to walk in the house.

She came back out-in the same sexy robe. "Is everything all right?" I asked her. "I just heard a lot of screaming and shit. I would hate to think your peoples put his hand on you or something. Hitting a woman is a real sucker move." I dug the knife in deeper.

"This is my son's father," she replied. "He was just a little upset over some bullshit that is not even his concern. He seems to think I bring men around my son. I told him I didn't."

"Main man, let me talk to you outside for a second," I said, taking charge. I motioned for him to come in the hallway. He came without hesitation-he was more of a sucker than I thought.

"Ma," I said, "don't worry about no nigger putting their hands on you. I'm just a knock away if that should happen. I will go back to the joint in a New York second over some nigger abusing a woman."

I had to let him know I just came home from jail and didn't mind going back and also let her know that she didn't have to worry about him being the one to do anything to her again, since he didn't have the heart to stand up to me.

She got the picture-I could see her nipples perk up.

Homeboy, meanwhile, was still waiting outside the door in the hallway. Nothing in the world couldn't convince me that he wasn't soft as a motherfucker. I wanted him to wait for a few more seconds so he would recognize I was exercising control over his ass.

I gave my set of instructions to "Sweetness" to

give to my aunt and then went out to the edge of the door to talk to her son's father. He looked so docile at that point; I wanted to smack the shit out of him for that alone.

(It's always some soft-ass nigger that will choose to scream on his girl the way he wouldn't scream on another nigger.)

I made it my business to get straight to the point with him. She was looking at me and I wanted her to see the directness of my approach and the firmness in my voice. In my mind, if anybody was going to control her, it was going to be me from here on out. I was applying the same ol' principles I had learned in prison. This bitch was going to owe me for this shit, whether she realized it or not.

I turned to her bitch of a son's father. "Main man," I said, "I can see soft all in your eyes. If I'm wrong, you're going to attempt to knock me out for making such a statement. The flipside to that is, what will I do to you for even trying it? What I need you to do is keep your hands off of her and be easy. You don't get no brownie points busting a woman in the mouth when you know in your heart of hearts you won't do it to a nigger. Especially a nigger like me.

"If I find out you have been mistreating her in anyway, I am going to come down on your ass like a ton of bricks. You feel me?"

He gave me this dumb look that suggested he accepted what I had just said as law and went back into the house like he'd just been pimp-smacked.

Sweetness was grinning from ear to ear.

"What's your name by the way?" I asked.

"It's Robin, but your aunt calls me Luscious. I guess you can call me Luscious, too; I like it better than Robin."

I gave her a peck on the cheek and went to the elevator feeling like the bad-ass nigger I was ordained to be. I knew her baby's father wouldn't dare say anything slick out of the mouth or do anything that would make me bust his shit, so I was comfortable leaving her with him.

Initially, I was going to take a cab uptown to my old 'hood, Lincoln Projects, but it was nice outside. What better way to waste some time than to walk from 111th Street to 135th and Fifth Avenue? I thought.

I was amazed at just how much Harlem had changed, in terms of its appearance. It wasn't the slum I remembered. I could see the benefits from Urban Renewal programs. Foster Projects, on 113th Street looked like it was fit for a king to live in now. They had beautiful windows and a hell of a landscape. There was even a neatly trimmed garden.

One hundred and sixteenth was bustling with commerce. There, the old Shabazz mosque was renovated to look like it came straight out of Egypt. Across from the mosque was a small marketplace with all kinds of African wares and products.

There were tour buses lined up on the downtown side of the street with "crackers" getting off. Shit must have changed. There was a time when crackers wouldn't come uptown-daytime or nighttime. The streets were no longer full of potholes; they were smoothly paved.

One hundred and twenty-fifth-couldn't help walking all the way up there-had the most dramatic facelift of all. On every corner there was a bank and an ATM machine. I had missed out on a lot of shit being locked down all of those years. Ten years ago that type of shit was unheard of. For one, niggers in Harlem didn't have any money to spend in the first place, and secondly, it was risky-motherfuckers would either target the banks or rob the people coming out of the ATM's.

Eighth Avenue had a brand new look with a Disney superstore and new Magic Johnson theatres. Magic Johnson built these theatres as a way of giving back to his community. (For the life of me, I couldn't see how it was "giving back" to the community; he stood to take more from it than what he was actually giving back ... in terms of hiring a few people to work there.)

I later found out he owned a Starbucks coffee shop on 125th and Lennox, an espresso shop to be exact. I always thought that type of shit was for rich folk, and here he got niggers paying seven dollars for a cup of coffee with sugar and whip cream in it.

Another sign to me that Harlem was indeed on the come up-there were billboards posted every-where. Even the Apollo had a facelift as well.

Strolling back across 125th Street to get to my projects, I bumped into an old-timer named Allen, a well-respected street photographer. He took pictures of all the ballers of Harlem. He would get exclusive invites to all of their parties so that he could take flicks of the who's who of the Harlem underworld.

* * *

Drug dealers, stick-up kids, and everyone in-between trusted Allen because he never showed anyone else their pictures; you paid for and received only the pictures you either told him to take of you, or were in with someone else, and he would never give anyone the negatives. You got an eight by ten photo for ten dollars. If you lost the picture or wanted additional copies, you would have to tell him the year and place of the party, and he would have a duplicate copy for you in a day or two.

Allen started out in the 60's as photographer for the Apollo, taking pictures of all of the performing acts and the famous people that graced its theatre. He would then dupe and sell these pictures-his side-hustle-on the streets of Harlem-dollar for a regular-size photo.

Allen threw a party for himself at the Apollo where he ran into Nicky Barnes. Nicky hired him to be his personal photographer for three hundred and fifty dollars a week-back then that was lawyer money. When Nicky went down on federal charges Allen was stuck on stupid because he had quit his gig with the Apollo.

After a bout with depression for a spell, he took to the streets and started taking pictures of moviegoers as they exited the old movie theatre, near the OTB building. When word got out about how elaborate his photo designs were he couldn't stop getting beeps from drug dealers, to do their parties and ghetto weddings. He had bamboo chairs with a phone prop so that you could act like you were on the phone while being photographed. He also had artists like Eric B and Rakim airbrushed with bed sheets as background.

* * *

It was really good seeing him. We chatted for a little while, and I gave him my aunt's number and headed uptown to my original destination. If I ever wanted to get back in the scene, I knew Allen was a good nigger to get me in the mix; he had contacts for days-I could get any baller's number I wanted from him because we were cool like that.

On the last stretch of my walk uptown, I couldn't help but stop at my old stomping grounds on 129th and Lennox. There was an old tenement ready to fall down that was dubbed "Castle Greyskull." You can get lost in that bitch. The building had all types of winding stairwells and back entrances and abandoned apartments. It had more crack houses in the building than any tenement in Harlem.

It was the one place I could go as a young stick-up kid and catch a "vic" at anytime of the day or night. I would catch a crackhead either coming in the building or in one of the "base" houses. I didn't care back then-if you had fifty dollars or fifty cents-I was taking it.

As a young nigger coming up in Harlem, full of cum, and a fetish for guns, it was hard for me not to get caught up in a life of crime. A gun made me feel like I was on even grounds with a six-foot, two hundred fifty-pound nigger. If I got the draw on you first, it didn't matter how big you was, because bullets don't respect size or height.

I tried to resist the temptation to go inside the building, but something inside of me was drawing me in. I was "geeking" to feel that rush that I had felt long ago, of sticking somebody up. To me, there was truly no feeling like pointing a gun at somebody's face and telling them what I would do to them if they were reluctant to give me what belonged to me. It belonged to me because I felt like, if you wasn't willing to die for it, then you didn't deserve it anyway.

As I walked into the building the smell of shit and rusted pipes hit my nostrils with a potency that could stop an elephant in its tracks. It brought back memories of ghetto grandeur, of a time when I could stick someone up for less than a hundred dollars and get fresh and go to the movies with change to spare. I was relapsing; I knew it was time to go.

I turned back around without even getting to the second floor. It only took the smell of a building to bring back my craving for the stick-up game. That's all it took to lose it all-a trigger, a few minutes to make a dumb-ass move before the next count time.

When I finally got to the front of the building, the air was just as intoxicating on my membranes. The only thing that bought me out of my nostalgic stupor was fresh air.

I double-timed back to the corner of Lennox Avenue and headed for Lincoln. When I got to the Mc Donald's on 132nd Street and Lennox, I made a right to Fifth Avenue to my projects. The old firehouse was still there, still abandoned. I don't even think people remembered that it was the old fire station. It had been abandoned since I was a kid.

It was amazing to see all of the revitalization projects going on in Harlem, and yet there were still buildings abandoned almost twenty years. When I was on the bus coming home I couldn't see the detail that I see now; the buildings looked the same from the bus, but now that I was up close and personal I was able to see just how much things changed.

The salon was still there, but it wasn't called "Ms. Claretta's" anymore. It was now "Ava's Beauty

Shop."

As I was walking by it, a voice rang out like a
siren calling my name. "Mike! Mike!"

When I turned around, there was a dude
standing in front of the shop door with a barber's covering on and one side of his head braided. At first I
didn't know who the fuck it was, but when I got close
up on him, I realized it was Polo, an old childhood
friend.

He directed me to come in the barbershop
while he was getting his hair done. I had to remember that I would encounter bouts of amnesia when it
came to recalling faces; after all, I was a kid when I
left. Shit! I guess if he could remember me, then how
hard could it really be?

When I got inside I could see that all eyes were
on me. I guess I had that "I-just-came-home-from-jail
look."

"Yo," he said, "this is where I get my hair done
at. Well, I guess that's obvious; I'm in the chair, right?
Ms. Claretta died three years ago, and her daughter
sold it to her." He pointed to a lady doing hair.

"Lynnette," he said, "I want you to meet my
man Mike from way back." Then he said to me,
"Mike, that's Lynette, the new owner."

"Nice to meet you," I said.

There were seven chairs, and he went down
the line introducing me to each person. I wasn't that
interested in meeting all of them, so as he was telling
me I zoned out his voice and gave back a generic,

"Nice to meet you."

The only person who caught my immediate attention was Lynette because she was the owner-and the two faggots doing hair.

The first one made it very clear who he was and what he wanted to be called. He said, "My name is Anthony, but everyone calls me Tony for short-that's t-o-n-i." I knew right then he was a blade runner and quite comfortable being one. The other one had an outright female name-Precious. I knew damn well Precious wasn't his given name; he wanted everyone to know he was proud to be flaming faggot of it.

They were both looking at me as if I was a piece of candy cane or something. In all honesty, I wasn't the least bit offended-I wasn't going to vocalize that. Shit, I knew bitches were feeling me just like the niggers was. I was a double threat. I was flattered. It was hard enough for niggers to get a bitch to really feel them and here I was getting play from both bitches and she-men.

I noticed a big red sign posted on the wall right next to the door: "Barbers Wanted." I was not trying to be nobody's barber; I was far too educated to relegate myself to cutting hair for the rest of my life.

Another reason I didn't want to work in that bitch-the way those faggots were looking at me. The last thing I wanted to do was to relapse, especially on the street with all of this ass out here just waiting for me to pluck something.

Even though I wasn't thinking about no faggot shit, those fags made me feel a little uneasy-I was getting hot flashes thinking about Dee Dee. That alone told me that I needed to get the fuck up out of there.

It's amazing how certain cues can trigger an old memory. It wasn't just those two-any homo would have probably triggered the thought of Dee Dee. And every time I thought about Dee Dee, it made it that much easier for me to bend my principles concerning homosexuality. Outwardly I was disgusted, but deep inside, within the core of my inner being, I was all right with the fact that I was thinking about a man like I was thinking about a woman.

I had to get the fuck out of there-and quick ... those "mo's" looking at me in the fashion that they were was starting to touch me in ways that I shouldn't express....

I gave Polo the number to my aunt's house and told him I would catch up with him. I held up my hand and waved to everyone in the salon and said, "Later yeah. And thanks for the hospitality. I'll be seeing you all again."

I made a beeline for the door and jetted across the street and vanished like a thief in the night into the blanket of high-rise project buildings that blocked me from the view of the people in the salon.

The projects were empty as a black hole. It was as if I was walking in the desert all by myself. Swarms of people used to be outside whenever I came up here-rain, sleet, or snow. The benches and the entranceways of buildings would be littered with people. It was so desolate now; if I whispered I could hear it across the street.

I didn't want to go to my mother's house, but I was all the way up here and no one was outside. So I figured-what the hell-I had to see her eventually. I might as well get this shit over with.

I reluctantly headed for my mother's building, situated on the corner of 133rd Street. It divided one side of the projects from the other. When I got inside of the building I soon realized that nothing really changed. The hallway floors were as nasty as ever, and the inside of the elevator was drenched in piss. My mother lived on the top floor in one of the short buildings. The apartment door was right next to the elevator, so you could hear and see everyone that came on the floor.

As I stepped off of the elevator I began to feel all of that pent-up anger from my mother not coming to visit me, or send me a postcard. I wanted to curse her out as soon as she opened the door. But how could you curse out the woman that gave you life?

I knocked on the door, trying to hold back any semblance of anger or hostility. I knocked on the door and stood there for a spell, waiting for a response, but none came. No one was home, not even my sister.

When I got downstairs in front of the building, my heart swelled with rage. She had the audacity not to be home on the day I was coming home. I was so

disgusted at my mother, I was sidetracked from
doing what I had come uptown to do-meet and greet.
She had let me down again, but that was okay. I was
not going to allow her to ever let it happen again.

I hailed a gypsy cab on 133rd and Madison
and went back downtown to my aunt's house. As I
thought about what had just happened to me, I wondered, Why should I be upset with her not being
there?-She wasn't there for me any other time.

An inner peace took over my body. I got out of
that cab feeling like everything was going to be all
right-with or without her.

My aunt was looking out the window when I
got in front of the building. I looked up and there she
was screaming at the top of her lungs, "Mikey!
Mikey!"

I hadn't heard that name since I was a kid; in
fact, she was the only one that called me that.

The door was wide open when I got off the
elevator. My little cousin came running out of the
door and leaped right into my arms. My aunt was
equally excited to see me. She started kissing me all
over the cheeks as she would do when I was a little
boy.

Her style of dress was still the same. She had
on an African head wrap and a long dress with an
embroidered African design that looked real tribal.

I glazed over the living room to see if there
were any items that would indicate that another adult
was present. I guess I wanted to believe my mother

wasn't home because she was down here waiting for me. So much for hopes and dreams.

My aunt's statement made it very clear to me where my mother was. "Your mother is in Brooklyn with her friend," she said, "Mr. Bodack. They're getting his stuff out of storage."

"Who is Mr. Bodack?" I asked, puzzled.

The look on her face assured me that this was information she thought I had. "Your mother obviously didn't tell you," she said. "She met a friend at rival service. I'm sure she will tell you when she sees you tonight."

Yeah, right, I thought to myself. As far as she was concerned, it probably wasn't my business to know.

My mother can be such a whore at times, always judging others but never herself. Always quick to tell someone about living in sin, and here it is she met a so-called Christian in church and they are about to shack up together. More power to her. I sure wasn't going to be around when she got here; I had more important things on my mind-like seeing Diane, the girl I met in the bank.

"Look, Aunty," I said, "I am going to make a few phone calls, and then I am going to catch the breeze. I'll see my mother another time.

"Take this money. Put two thousand away for me, and you take two thousand. I appreciate and love you more than you will ever know."

Her eyes lit up like a reefer joint in a dark

room. "Where did you get all of this money?" she asked.

"I was saving while I was incarcerated; they pay you a little something, you know."

She knew that you got paid for working in prison because I would send her two's and fews and the check would be from the institution, from me. I didn't dare tell her what I was doing or how I got all of that cash.

She took the dough and stuffed it in her bra. I gave my cousin a crispy fifty-dollar bill and headed straight for the phone. I wanted to be "ghost" before my mother even thought about getting here. Something told me I should have stuck around, but I knew my aunt would understand. Shit! I just got out of prison-she knew a nigger was going to be antsy on his first day out.

I pulled Diane's number out of my back pocket and dialed. The phone rang several times before an answering machine came on. Just as I was leaving a message, someone picked up the phone. "Hello, hello."

"Hello, is this Diane?" The words got caught between my throat and my chest cavity.

Her voice changed a bit when she realized it was a man; it was softer and sweeter. "This is she. Who's calling?"

"This is Michael. We met earlier in the bank, I'm the guy that cashed the nine-thousand-dollar check."

Her voice perked up. "Oh yeah! What's up? I didn't expect you to call me."

"I just got home and I wanted to go out. I would love to come and get you, and me and you can have a good time tonight."

"Well," she said after a five-second delay, "I was already going out with my girlfriends, but I guess I can break it off and make an exception. Take my address down."

"Wait. Let me get a pen."

"It's 539 Lennox Avenue."

I wrote it down on a matchbook near the phone. That was right near Harlem Hospital. I knew that because Harlem Hospital was 500 Lennox.

(When I was a kid we called Harlem Hospital 500 Hope Avenue because if you went in for anything you better hope you come out. You could go in with a common cold and come out with tuberculosis.)

She said she lived on the third floor, 3F to be exact, and I told her I would be there in a few.

If it wasn't the first time I was getting up with her, I would have suggested we skip the going out and get right to the fucking and sucking, but I knew she wasn't that type of girl just by her demeanor. Besides, I needed to get out anyway; fucking and sucking was going to be around forever and a day as long as I was on the street.

My aunt knew what time it was the moment I got off the phone. That's what I loved about her-she knew how to give you your space and be there for you all in the same breath. She let me know that she would keep the chain off, and to put it on when I got in. I kissed her and my cousin and bolted out the door.

I jumped in a cab and shot uptown to her crib. She lived in a short tenement building on the downtown side of 137th Street, a building connected to a check cashing place and an Arab store. It was much cleaner than I had expected, given the neighborhood. The building was also without an intercom. I simply walked upstairs and knocked on her door.

On her door was one of those Greek sorority emblems in pink with lavender trim. She opened the door and I was hit with a soft female fragrance that matched her femininity.

She gave me a tour of her one-bedroom apartment. There was wall-to-wall plush carpet everywhere. The living room carpet was beige with matching furniture, and the dining room table and chairs were made of dark redwood.

Her academic accomplishments hung on all four sides of her walls. She had a bachelor's of science from the University of Maryland, Eastern Shore, and a masters of science in organizational management from Spelman. There were pictures of her frat brothers and sorority sisters on her wall unit. On the hallway wall leading to her bedroom were plaques with different prayers inscribed on them.

Her bathroom was decked out in her sorority colors. When you stepped over the threshold of her bathroom, you were greeted with a pre-recorded chant of her sorority sisters making the hissing meow sound of a feline.

In her bedroom she had a waterbed with teddy bears placed on the headboard. The room had an Egyptian theme to it with a picture of Nefertiti and the words, "Women rule," over the bed.

I was ushered back into the living room area with her holding my hand. She sat me on the couch and came back from the kitchen with glasses and an opened bottle of red wine. I had never had wine before, but I had read wine-tasting books in prison. So I pretty much knew how to hold the wine glass and enjoy the aroma.

Sipping on the wine, the first thing came to my mind was, How in the fuck could she afford to hook up her apartment on her salary? And more importantly, Why was she working as a teller with all of those academic credentials?

"Ma, you are much too educated to be working as a teller in a bank. What's your angle?"

She looked at me and started laughing. "I was waiting for you to get around to asking me that. My father is actually the bank president. He told me if I wanted to someday be a bank president I would have to learn every facet of the business, and so I'm starting from the ground up."

"Where you from?"

"Originally from Hempstead, Long Island. I came to Harlem and fell in love with the people.

When I was growing up, I was one of only five blacks in my school, so the first chance I got to get the hell out of there I took it. That's why I went to black colleges."

That shit shut me up real quick. Not to mention, I was starting to see dollar signs. This broad was going places, and she was fine as hell on top of it.

I was getting tipsy from all the wine I was ingesting. I didn't realize it until she had looked at her watch-we were rapping and yapping for well over two hours.

She told me it was time to head out for the club. We were to meet her friends outside because they had VIP tickets.

When we got downstairs, I tried to wave a cab. She put a halt to that real quick. Out in front was a white limited-edition Range Rover with chrome rims and a crash bar. When I saw her point to it with a little black object in her hand and the lights came on, I soon realized that she was no cab-type broad. I did glance at it on my way upstairs, but I wouldn't have in a million years assumed that it was her ride.

When I got in the joint I felt like I was living the life of a rock star or something. She had DVD and TV's in the headrest and a dropdown screen in the middle, between the front and back seats. When she turned the ignition, the DVD came on. Superfly was playing. I recognized it from the scene where Superfly was in the bathtub with that fine-ass black woman.

As I watched the scene I began to play a visual of me and her acting out that same scene. The sudsy water glistened on her butt cheeks, and he passionately tongue-kissed her. I thought to myself, If I ever got a chance, I was going to fuck her the same way-nice, slow and passionate.

It was dark outside and the night seemed to blend in with the mood and atmosphere in the car. Every so often she took her eye off the road to gaze at me, and feeling her looking at me, I would return the favor. There was a magic to the whole scene that assured me I was coming back to her place, when all was said and done.

We arrived at the club-"Webster Hall"-in star-studded fashion. All eyes were on her and the ride. She had to be a regular. Her friends came rushing to the car before we could even get to a complete and slipped her the tickets-we went in without even having to wait on line.

You could hear the music from the door. The club was dimly lit, strobe lights everywhere. I slipped her two hundred dollars and told her, "Get drinks for you and your friends; I gonna mingle around the club for a minute."

She looked impressed by that.

I didn't want to be up in her and her girl-friends' face all night-like some crab.

There were three levels to the club. The first floor played house music, the second, reggae, and the third, hip hop. I guess the owners figured out quick, if those rowdy hip hop niggers get crazy, the sensible party goers on the two floors below had ample time to get the fuck out before they started killing up everybody.

I didn't really know how to dance but I was going to mingle like I had partied all of my life. I went from floor to floor like I knew the scene. The hip hop floor was jumping off to my liking. There was phat bitch-hoes and niggers busting bottles everywhere.

Across from me I saw this Spanish cat with a long ponytail hanging busting bottles and passing out drinks like there was no tomorrow. I knew that ponytail from anywhere. I walked up to the cat and tapped him on the shoulder.

He turned around and greeted me with an instant hug and kiss on the cheek like he knew me all of his natural life. It was Rico-Tislam's bitch. He was obviously in pole position on the street. He hadn't changed one bit. The only thing changed was that he looked like a whole lot of money.

He told me he was moving big weight out of Queens with some black dudes-he called them over to introduce them one by one. He said they called themselves the "Gangster Unit," from Southside Jamaica, Queens.

A short, stocky one introduced himself as

"Half-a-dollar."

What kind of name was "Half-a-dollar"?

Half-a-dollar's partners were "Stop the bank" and "Young God."

All of that shit sounded crazy to me.

Rico said they were pushing massive amounts of that white powder for him and that he was seeing near a hundred grand a week from all of his operations.

I hugged the shit out of him without even allowing him to explain any further. I wanted him to know that it was love from the jump-shit! he had paper.

He handed me a business card. "If you want to get on, give me a call," he said. "I had an initiation that was required of every man that got down with me … so if you call, be prepared."

I was a little confused. Nonetheless, I took his card and started to float around the club again.

I couldn't help thinking about seeing Rico and how well he was doing on the street. But I didn't care; I didn't want to take that route.

I went back downstairs to see what Diane was doing with her friends. They were down there dancing and hugging each other like they were lovers or something. Maybe it was just my interpretation of what I saw.

I cut in between Diane and one of her friends, to take my rightful place with her. After that, it was a wrap. We danced damn-near the whole night away. I just knew I was getting some pussy tonight. It wouldn't have mattered if I didn't-I was feeling her anyway; it was just the way the night was unfolding.

When the lights came on, I knew it was the last song-"Computer Love." In the middle of the song, I started to kiss her on the lips to see how far I could go. She let me put my tongue in her throat; it was on from there. I knew I was boning.

We walked out of the club holding hands like two lovebirds in a tree. Thank God, her friends didn't "cock-block" by asking for a ride uptown or some shit. We jumped in the car and headed uptown via the FDR Drive, laughing and joking all the way. Once we passed the 96th Street exit I knew I was not going home either. She could have easily dropped me off, but she wanted me to come back to her place just as bad as I wanted to go there.

As we got off the 135th Street exit I started prepping her mind, body and soul for what I wanted to do to her once we got upstairs-assuming, of course, I got up there. She could be intending to let me out in front of her building since I met her there to go to the club.

"When we get in I want to practice some of my French arts with you. You feel me?"

"Oh yeah? What's that?" She gave me a look of puzzlement of what I meant by "French arts" and not whether or not we were going up.

"I'll show you when I get upstairs"-I was in like Flynn-"you won't be disappointed."

The spot that she had left in front of the building was still vacant. I got out of that truck faster than a speeding bullet.

I began to feel on her ass as we walked upstairs. All I could think about was sticking my rod deep inside her. As soon as the door to her apartment opened I commenced to taking off her clothes like a reckless wild animal.

She put her moneymaker in my face and signaled for me to go down for a taste. Without hesitation, I started licking on her caboose and slightly pinching her bell peppers, until she began to moan with excitement.

Her body was my globe, and I was going to travel all around the world. I turned her around and came in from the backdoor so that she couldn't see what I was holding right away-she was going to be shocked two times when she felt my throbbing delivery from the back.

I parted those buttermilk biscuits and slid my "love-stick" in for the homerun. She was as lubricated as ball bearing oil in a car.

We fucked and sucked the whole night away. I didn't even know I had that long in me. When she felt the pulse of my semen coming down she took my champagne flute in her hand and began to suck the cocoa butter-colored liquids right out of it.

I had to see if she would let me top the night off with a little ass-shot. I took some saliva out of my mouth and placed it gently on my breeder's cock, to go for the "brown."

She didn't resist a bit.

I inched my head in first and then began to push for the goal line inch by inch, until everything but the base of my cock was deep within her "doonkie" chute. Our bodies were so close together and so intertwined, I could feel the blood in her veins moving up and down her body cavity.

That night was as blissful as the feeling I felt when I first penetrated Dee Dee-I was longing for that deep, tight hole and was enjoying every minute of being inside her from behind.

It was a revelation to me: I was in love with the brown trout. And it all started one day in the shower with a nigger named Dee Dee. I knew that this wasn't going to be the first time, nor the last.

For me, man or woman, it didn't matter-as long as I got a piece of some good asshole I was completely satisfied. After hours of just laying there with my magic wand stuck deep inside her, I pulled out, rolled over and went to the land where dreams meet reality.

CHAPTER THIRTEEN

I had been on the streets for a couple of months with no success at finding gainful employment-no one would hire me because of my criminal record. I decided that today was going to be my last day trying to make it right by being a productive citizen in society.

Diane was trying the best she could to get her father to hire me in whatever capacity he could, but he wasn't budging.

Every now and then I would go into Ava's Beauty Shop and cut a few heads, but I wasn't really feeling it. It started with a few days, as a favor, to keep parole off of my back.

I was getting cool with everyone in the shop, especially Precious and Toni. I knew they wanted me to fuck the shit out of them, but I wasn't paying that any mind. They kept trying to invite me to this club across the bridge called "the Quarry." I had heard from the other girls in the shop that that wasn't the type of club to be fucking around in. I kept putting Precious and Toni off, week after week.

I felt a degree of loyalty to both of them because they both would give me paper every chance they got. It was as if they were baiting me so that I could bless them with some dick. They had no idea I had "dabbled" in prison, so I had no reason to believe they were acting out of some prior knowledge about me; they just had a craving for me and thought they might have a shot if they were nice to me.

All faggots get off trying to turn somebody out that they believe is straight-it's the only way to validate their sexuality, I thought.

The money I had come home with was gone the week after I got out. Me and Diane was partying like it was 1999. My aunt knew I was fucked up and started giving me the money back in small pieces every morning before I left for a job interview or to canvass for one. When I woke up this morning, there was a note on the table with some Hi Ho crackers, and a fifty-dollar bill wishing me luck on my search today.

This was it for me-I was tired of the let-downs. I went outside and got a Daily News when I got dressed. I was going to hit as many job agencies as possible.

Every agency I went to made me fill out a long questionnaire. I wouldn't even make it past the next phase because the moment they saw the box checked off about me having a felony conviction, they would come up with an excuse why I wasn't a right fit.

I thought there were laws against shit like

that? I walked all the way downtown by City Hall, canvassing the whole of the city on foot. I was home only a few months and was still appreciating my freedom. I saw a sign directly in the back of city hall that read, "New York City Housing Authority is looking for you."

I decided to go in and have a look-see. Maybe they were looking for me. I went upstairs to the housing administration floor. It was packed with niggers waiting to be seen for an interview.

I was the only nigger there with a suit on and resumé in hand. I knew I was on my way. I went up to the front desk.

"Are you here for the employment fair for housing?" the receptionist asked.

"Yes, ma'am, I am."

"Then I am going to need you to fill out this application, and when your name is called follow the green line to the door that says 'Interview.' "

I filled it out and returned it to her and was called about half an hour later. I followed the green line and saw the sign in front of a lady's office-Mrs. Delaney, a beautiful black woman with luscious big lips that you would just want to kiss all over.

"Mr. Fraser," she said, "I looked over your application and I see you have an associate's degree in liberal arts and a bachelor's in business administration. Are you sure you're applying for the right job?"

"The maintenance position is perfect for me right now, Mrs. Delaney."

"I mean there are other positions in our organization that can accommodate and utilize your skills."

I am thinking to myself, I know this, but I wanted to shoot low, to give them no reason to tell me no. "As you can see, I am more than qualified to sweep floors and mop hallways."

"Well, I guess that settles that," she said, astonished. "When can you start?"

"As soon as possible."

"Okay then. Be at this address on Monday morning, 9:00 a.m. sharp."

"Thank you, ma'am. Thank you very much." I was excited as hell; I had landed a job.

Just as I reached the door—"Oh, Mr. Fraser, I'll just need you to sign here and check box number sixteen."

Shit, I knew it was too good to be true.

We all know what box number sixteen was. I hesitantly took the application and checked off yes and handed her back the application.

She looked it over, and her expression changed. "Mr. Fraser, I'm very sorry, but the city's policies state that any individual hired for a city agency position must have a clean record."

"Mrs. Delaney," I pleaded, "what am I supposed to do? If the city doesn't want to hire me, what can I expect from the private sector?"

"Mr. Fraser, I'm sorry, but those are the rules and policies set. I'm so sorry."

"Yeah, me too."

I turned my back on her in disgust and headed out of the office. I felt like Al Pacino in "The Godfather"-the more I tried to get out of the life of crime, the more I was inadvertently being pulled back in.

If no one was going to give me a chance, then I was going to take a chance and create the American dream for myself. No way I was going to starve out here.

I went to a pay phone on the corner in front of the building and decided to pull out my ace in the hole: Rico's number. I was holding back because I thought I could make it without doing the wrong thing; I was sadly mistaken.

Crime was my only option at this point, and if I was going to venture back, I might as well do it with all of my heart.

On the other end of the receiver was the voice I needed to hear. It was Rico's.

"Yo, Ric, it's your boy, Black," I said, "from the penal. You gave me your number a couple of months ago with an offer to make things happen if I wanted in. Well, now I want in."

"My nigger, this is your lucky day. We have an initiation in about two hours at "the spot." Can you make it?"

I was thinking to myself, what kind of initiation? but I was so desperate I was down for whatever. "Yeah, I can make it," I said. "Just give me the address."

"It's 950 West 120th Street."

"I'm heading up there right now," I told him.

I jumped on No. 6 train to Times Square, took the shuttle to the A train, and headed uptown. I got off at 125th Street, one block from Eighth Avenue.

When I got out of the station, I pulled out the paper with the address-it was within walking distance-and headed down Morningside Avenue.

When I got to 120th Street I realized I was already in the 900's. What type of operation was he running in one of these houses?

The building was a nice-looking brownstone. I knocked on the door and someone came to the peephole and gave me this piercing look. "Who?" someone yelled.

"It's Michael. Is Rico there?"

There was a slight pause. The peephole slid shut, and several locks were unlocked. The door flew open and Rico stood there looking like he was welcoming someone he hadn't seen in a lifetime.

My mind flashed back to the times when we were kids in Sparford and this young Puerto Rican let Tislam fuck the shit out of him. I thought about how weak he was then and how strong he seemed now-you could see he was no sucker. I didn't see an ounce of punk in him; in fact, I saw nothing but strength ... from the level of respect his comrades had for him.

I wondered, how could that be, if they know his past and what happened to him as a kid, and probably as an adult?

He yelled, "Mike!"

I jolted back to reality. "Yeah, it's me in the flesh," I said.

He took me into the house where the rest of his homeboys were. We went to a side-room where he wanted to discuss some things with me before he re-introduced me to the rest of his clique-I had met three of them Gangster Unit niggers at Webster Hall my first night home.

Rico's eyes looked as if he was bracing to tell me something. "We have an initiation," he said, "that ensures every man down with us keeps a secret. It is a secret that can ruin any man and is shared by all of us, so no man is above the crew-I thought of it. It is also a way for me to hide the sin of what Tislam done to me back in the day.

"Every nigger down with us has to fuck some-body in the crew and has to get fucked by all of us in the crew. In doing so, we have something on you, and you have something on us. We are all men by virtue of our shared secret. What someone can know about you, they can also know about me. You telling on someone in the crew is like telling on yourself."

"Are you fucking crazy?" I asked. "Do you think I would even entertain letting somebody fuck me up the ass?"

"You are definitely welcome to leave and there is no hard feelings. But I got a move that we all are about to make that is going to set all of us straight for the rest of our lives-and oh yeah!-don't think I don't know what you were doing while you were on lockdown. I know Dee Dee real well. He was down with us before he died. He told me all about you."

I was stunned. "You know what," I said, "I am not even going to lie about it; I need to get it out in the open anyway. You know how it is on lockdown: I just wanted to feel the touch of a woman, and Dee Dee was the closest thing to one. I kept your secret a secret, and I hope you can keep mine."

"Dog, I didn't bring it up because I am no better than you as a man. I got fucked as a kid but I am still a man. I don't have any ill feelings for Tislam; in a lot of ways he taught me how to be strong.

"I do think you are missing out on an opportunity to get some real paper, but once again, rules are rules. So ... if you want to get down, I suggest you think about it."

Shit! What real choice did I have? I didn't have shit, and my cover was blown; I might as well get something out of the deal.

I had to know one thing though-it was killing me: "What happened to Dee Dee?" I asked. "How did he die?"

Rico looked down with sadness. "Pneumonia."

What a relief! I thought to myself. At least it wasn't AIDS.

"I am going to take you up on your offer," I said, "but whatever the move is, I want to call the shots. I think I can do a better job than those dudes I saw you with at the club that night I came home."

"A'ight, you got that. Now let me take you inside."

He took me to a smoke-filled room with dudes sitting at a round table, like the knights in King Arthur's court. Some were smoking; others were counting mounds of cash; some were putting vials of crack into plastic bags.

"Listen up, my niggers," Rico said. "I want to introduce y'all to a long-time homey of mine-he is like bone of my bone, and flesh of my flesh."

I looked at him from the corner of my eye.

"He's a G from the heart, and we can all learn a lot from him. Mike-this is the clique."

I give them a short, "What's up."

A kid-Murder Rob-was loading bullets with his bare hands. I had to let him know there was a brighter way to his madness.

"My man," I said, "try doing that with gloves; it works."

"Yo, see what I told y'all motherfuckers." Rico threw his arms around my shoulders. "He knows his shit!" He continued his introduction around the room. "You already know Half-a-dollar, Young God, and Stop the bank."

There were other niggers there he didn't even bother to introduce me to.

"Take off your clothes," he said to me, pulling a blindfold out of his pocket.

"What the fuck am I being blindfolded for?" I thought it was some sort of set-up-type shit going into play.

"The blindfold is so you don't know which one of us is fucking you-that way no one is above or below anyone else. All you will ever know is that you've been fucked in the presence of all who are present-it could be all of us fucking you, or just one."

The blindfold was then placed over my eyes, and I was led to another room. They bent me over a table and dropped my pants to below my knees.

There was nothing but silence for about two minutes. All of a sudden I feel this slippery substance being placed all over the crack of my ass, some sort of lubricant-then the sensation of a warm, thick object penetrating my anus.

After several pumps, I knew it was a stiff cock in my ass. I could feel the person's balls banging against my buttocks as he dug deeper and deeper into my guts.

More than one person was drilling me-I could feel the different placement of the balls on my body. Some were higher up on my ass than others, indicating the person was taller or shorter.

I was enjoying the unthinkable. As each person took turns sticking his dirty gun in my "shitter-chute," I could feel the blood pulsating through their venomous cocks and the sensation of a cool rush of menthol-injected spring waters.

This was my first game in the outfield as a catcher, but I knew it wouldn't be my last. This was my coming-out day, the day I admitted to myself that

I had a thing for that "manwich meal." I wasn't flaming; I was just infatuated with that Polish sausage. That one-eyed Cyclops had me right where he wanted me. At that moment there was no room for shame. I was a switch-hitter.

Everyone had their pants back on when the blindfold came off-I could never be able to tell which nigger just served the shit out of me.

There was a dick that I was sure to remember-his balls touched the groove of my back; he had to be tall.

Rico then told all of them to line up on the ball. I was to pick three of them to fuck, to complete my initiation. I chose the three Gangster Unit niggers.

I started with the short one, Half-a-dollar. He had a half-dollar tattooed on his back, and his mouth looked funny as hell. (I later learned he was shot nine times at close range for some shit he had nothing to do with. He wore those bullet holes like a badge of honor.) I bent him over the table and began pumping the shit out of him. He was as straight-faced as the character Denzel Washington played in Glory, when he was being beaten.

I knew he was doing it not because he liked it, but because it was the rules. If he was a woman, he would be considered a dead lay.

My next victim was his right-hand man-Stop the bank. He had a reserved, laid-back kind of look, a fake tough-guy façade; he just wasn't believable-that was the main reason I chose him. If I had to have anything on anybody, it was going to be him. I made it my business to not only fuck the shit out of him, but to cum in him as well.

Young God was the best fuck. He was light in the ass with a six-pack that gave me a good visual to work with. I made him get on the table and hold his dick while I lifted up his legs and fucked him from the front. When I was done, I squirted all over his stomach. He looked at me with disgust, but I didn't care. What was he going to do to me?

The initiation process not only allowed me to get down with them; it was also a way for me to test the waters of homosexuality without fear of reprisal. If I was a homo, it was going to be on my terms. I was going to be as thuggish as any nigger that ever walked on two feet.

Rico came over to me with a white cloth with something inside: a gold-plated dagger with the inscription, "Dagger of Honor."

"There is only one way to get out of this organ-ization," he said. "It's either going to be shit on my dick, or blood on a nigger's knife.

"No one man is above the crew. There is no one more important to each other more than the peo-ple in this room ... not mother, father, sister, nor son. We fuck together, kill together, and die together. Those that oppose us-fuck 'em two times, literally and figuratively."

This nigger was really on some shit, I thought. I could see a change in Rico that I knew had come from his experience with Tis. He was hell-bent on humiliating a motherfucker and couldn't even recognize it.

I was taken back to the room where the round table was and briefed on his so-called one-shot deal, to get out of the game.

I took a seat by the door. "Prison instincts," I guess-I was going to be the first one in and the first one out, should anything jump off.

When everyone sat down, Rico took center stage and explained his master plan. "A'ight, here's the deal. It's no secret we all said we wanted to get out of the game and into something more legitimate and suited to our characters.

"Half and his G Unit crew have been making moves on the industry, trying to break in as a rap group. I figure we could do this last big sting and front them the money to do it for themselves. We will all be equal partners with the label.

"I guess the question to ask is, where are we going to get the money to start a full-scale label to compete with the big labels? The answer is simple: Those guineas in little Italy are planning on hitting a selected group of dealers with over fifty kilos of heroin. Not coke-heroin.

"I can't even count the profit we will make off of some shit like that. It will be enough for all of us to live and start this legitimate enterprise. We could wash that money in no time by starting film companies, clothing lines, vodka and beer distributorships

… and anything else we can get our people to believe in.

"I got an inside flunky on their payroll-he gave me the names of the niggers they're going to hit off. If we rob these niggers and sell the drugs wholesale out of town, we will still make a killing."

"How do you expect us to do that without bringing all types of heat on ourselves?" I asked. "If anybody is giving anybody work like that, they have to believe they can hold it down."

"That's all the more reason I need you down on this," Rico said. "You got the mind for pulling it all together. One way or another, this is going to happen."

I could see he didn't really think things through. I gave him an E for effort, but an A for balls … for even thinking about a move like this. I was in-I had nothing to lose-but only if it went down with me mapping it out.

"First," I said, "I am going to need all the information you can get on these cats that they about to hit off: hang-out locations, places of residence, everything."

Then I gave him my aunt's address and told him to holler at me whenever he had it. We embraced, and I rolled out.

Exhausted from being up since early that morning, when I got back home to my aunt's house, I headed straight for my bed.

I lay there and stared at the ceiling. Then it

dawned on me that I had just let a nigger take the only thing from me that was sacred-my manhood. I was struggling with how to view myself, especially since I had grown up despising faggots for their "crimes."

I also started to think about the awful situation I was putting Diane in. She was now trapped in my web of deceit.

What penetrated my mind the most was that fateful day that started it all, changing my whole world forever. The day I wanted a nigger's belongings so bad I did the unthinkable to get it. I began to feel empty and confused.

Just as I was about to fade into dreamland, my aunt knocked on the door. "Mikey," she said, "someone name Rico is at the door for you."

"Thanks, aunty. I'll get it." I went to the door, and there was Rico with long white paper in his hand that looked like blueprints. I stepped in the hallway and pulled the door behind me, so my aunt wouldn't be privy to my business.

"This is everything you asked for and some," Rico said. "Yo, I even got their shit schedules. Mike, I got to take care of something, so here you go. Handle your business. I'll check you tomorrow, same bad place, same bad time."

I re-entered the apartment and locked the door behind me. I headed directly to my room, closed the door, and spread the paperwork on my bed so I could get an overall view of what I had in my possession.

The page had four names on it: Fat Jack, Chad, Ronnie, and Lynn. I glanced through the pages, got out a pen, and started taking notes on the information I had in front of me.

Right away, I noticed distinct patterns in all of them. Fat Jack, for example, never left the game room-he sold weight from there. Hitting at the right time would yield cash and drugs in abundance.

Chad was a flamboyant old-timer who could be seen on any given day strolling up and down 125th Street, looking for attention and affirmation of who he was. That made it that much easier to get him.

Ronnie was a young hustler who loved motor-cycles and cars. He could be found in one or the other.

Lynn was the tricky one. He never left his house-that made him easy to find-but a man in his own environment was dangerous.

I called Rico after I came up with a workable plan and told him to meet me with all his boys at their spot in the morning.

CHAPTER FOURTEEN

I woke up early the following morning. This time it was not to look for a job, but to do a job. This move was going to allow me to really do my aunt right, especially since I hadn't spent any real time with her since coming home.

When I got outside in front of the building, the weather was so nice I decided to walk all the way uptown across all the avenues up 112th Street to Morningside Avenue.

On the way I encountered none other than Detective Hartsfield, the arresting officer in my case. He had one of those faces that you couldn't forget. He seemed to have a hard-on for me now that I was much older and on the street. He pulled up alongside me in a maroon classic Capri. "Hey, Mikey," he mocked, "you found a job yet … or are you really looking? You may have gotten older, but you're the same ol' little juvenile delinquent from not so long ago."

"Are you finished, detective?"

"No, are you finished?-that is the question.

Don't think you're going to fuck up my streets anymore than what they are ... 'cause I'll be watching
you. You hear me?"

I kept my eyes fixated on him but didn't
respond. I started to walk away.

"Keep your eyes on the prize, Michael."

I sucked my teeth and kept moving.

When I reached the spot, everyone was there
waiting for me.

I laid the set of altered blueprints I had
received from Rico across the table. "What you have
here before you," I said, "is the exact way this operation is to go down ... on paper. In order for it to work
successfully, you'll have to execute it to the letter. I
have the formula to get the maximum out of the situ-
ation-I focused on their weaknesses rather than their
strengths.

"This guy, Fat Jack, never leaves the game
room, which means the stash is there also. Three of
you will be responsible for getting the "work" and
locking him up in there. Take out all the phones and
gag him, and leave the rest to me."

As I was describing the way events should
unfold, I could see all of them gesturing, forming
mental images.

"This guy Chad," I continued, "is out in the
public eye like Gotti or something. He feels protected
around the people. He'll have to be taken in the open-
no two ways about that; I prefer when he gets his
morning coffee and hash browns from Copeland's.

Why? Because less people are there in the morning.

"Bring him directly to the spot, and don't answer any questions. Put the child lock on the doors so he can't get out from the inside. In terms of Ronnie ... I got plans for him. Rico, you can come with me to handle that.

"I want to make sure you understand me clearly: Don't take nothing from these niggers but the drugs and the money. I mean nothing else."

I suggested to the Gangster Unit niggers-I sent them to handle Fat Jack-that they use the two meterman uniforms on the floor to gain access behind his locked doors. They all seemed to have a deeper bond that went far beyond that "crew shit" they had with everybody else.

The morning was still young, but I wanted them to roll in time to catch all of them. I had to make room for them fucking up; after all, they didn't know me that well, and I sure wasn't trusting them to be on point.

No sooner did me and Rico get halfway to our destination when he got a call on his cell phone from Half-a-dollar with the rundown on what was going on inside Fat Jack's joint.

Apparently, they got in without a hitch. His man Young God simply knocked on the door that separated the customers from himself and flashed a bogus ID.

***

Once the door was opened, it was obvious that letting him in was the wrong thing to do. Young God pulled out a .45 with a silencer on it and shot the doorman in the stomach. He went down, while Jack looked on, shitting bricks and begging for his life.

YG let Bank and Half in. Fat Jack realized he was at the end of the road. YG hit him with the butt of the gun and staked his claim. "A'ight, motherfucker, you know what this is! Don't start no shit and there won't be none."

"God, don't kill me," Fat Jack begged. "Please don't kill me!"

"Shut the fuck up," YG yelled. "You wasn't crying, selling that ounce you just sold a minute ago."

"Look, take the money," Jack offered. "It's under the freezer right there. It don't mean nothing to me; I got a daughter I want to see grow up."

"Then if you would be so kind as to tell me where the work is," said YG, "I think you gonna live to see her graduate."

"What 'work'?"

YG was ticked. "Now that's the wrong answer! Try again."

Fat Jack is now bleeding from the mouth. "Man, I'm telling you, the work is finished. I sold the last-"

"Bingo!" Bank yelled, holding two large ziplock bags full of dope. "I hit the jackpot."

"You lied to me, fat ass!" YG was boiling. "What have I done to deserve this disrespect?" he asked, looking at his boys for some feedback on the next move.

"Tie his ass up," Half-a-dollar said, "and take him to the back. Make sure he's tied tight."

Half-a-dollar, meanwhile, was ripping the phones out and yelling for them to hurry up.

They locked Jack in the back and shut the gate down as they exited. Then they all jumped in the car to head back to the spot to drop off what looked like two kilos of heroin before snatching Chad.

They were in the car discussing the situation. "I don't know about y'all," YG grinned, "but these two bricks of dope we got is a lot to smile about-we got over a million dollars in our possession."

"Fuck that," Half-a-dollar spat. "Right now I'm thinking about the stupid shit we just did."

"Did you hear what that man just said?" Bank asked, looking at Half-a-dollar as if he was crazy or something. "'We got over a million dollars in our possession.' Don't nothing sound fucked up about that."

YG turned to Half-a-dollar. "Yeah, nigger, you trippin' right now. Open the window and catch your breath."

"We just left a motherfucker alive that had over a million dollars worth of work," Half-a-dollar said. "Fuck that-turn around."

"Nigger, you stone-cold crazy!" YG looked at

him in utter shock.

"Turn around, yo," Half insisted. "We going to do this my way. I ain't leaving no bogeyman around to haunt me later."

"Our instructions were to tie him up and leave him alive," Bank reminded him.

"Fuck those instructions," Half-a-dollar yelled. "I'm not feeling taking no orders from no Johnny-come-on-the-spot. Turn the fuck around now!"

They reluctantly turned around and headed back for the candy store.

"Give me the keys and stay right here," Half ordered. "I'll be right out."

Half went inside and shot Jack twice in the head and relieved him of his Rolex. Then he came back out and got in the car.

"Now was that hard?" he asked as they drove off.

"Yeah, you damn right," YG responded. "Now we got a body that could have been taken care of by someone else."

"Yeah, whatever," Half said. "We got bodies anyway; one more ain't gonna kill us."

* * *

Uptown in Parkchester, a quiet suburban environment away from the 'hood, me, Rico, and his man stood in front of Ronnie's house, waiting for the right moment to run up in there on his ass.

Rico had binoculars and was getting a bird's-eye view of his crib: Ronnie was in the house with a bitch, getting his dick sucked. He had on a robe, and she was as naked as the day she was born.

"Dam!" exclaimed Rico, "that bitch can swallow a dick!"

"Let me see," his man said, snatching the binoculars from him. "Now that's a fine-looking asshole. Ugly niggers get all the good pussy when they got money."

"Let me see for a second," I said. "It's on-now is a better time than ever to roll up in there. I hope we catch him busting a nut."

The three of us got out of the car and approached the house from the back. Instead of breaking any doors or anything, we used electronic scramblers to pen the garage door and enter the house.

Rico tripped over an electrical cord, making a little noise.

"Shhh," I whispered. "You want him to know we're here?"

We went upstairs and came down to the living room area where Ronnie was freaking off. He was fucking her in the ass.

"Ooh! Fuck me, daddy," she groaned. "Cum inside me."

"I hope it felt good to you like it did for me," I

said, walking into the living room and pointing the
gun at Ronnie.

He reached for his gun on the nightstand by
him.

Was he crazy? "Now don't you go making a
bad situation worse," I said. "Get your motherfucking
hands up!-you too, bitch. Rico, get his gun; he is not
going to need it."

Rico recovered the gun from the nightstand,
and I signaled for Rico's man to put a set of handcuffs
on Ronnie, who couldn't figure it all out.

"I don't know what the fuck this is all about,"
Ronnie said, "but if you disappear in five minutes I'll
forget this little incident ever happened."

We all started laughing at that shit.

"You can forget from now until Armageddon,"
Rico teased. "Reality will help jog your memory,
'cause we ain't going nowhere."

"What the fuck do you want-money? I'll give
you ten thousand apiece?"

"We don't just want money," Rico explained;
"we want a cut from all your legitimate operations
and we want to be plugged in to your guinea
friends."

I was taken aback by that. I thought the plan
was to get the money and get the fuck out of the
game. It sounded to me like Rico had an agenda alto-
gether different from what we discussed.

I was more concerned about the money and
the drugs. Nonetheless, I had to roll with it because I

didn't want to show dissent in front of Ronnie.

"Now you know I can't do that," Ronnie said; "that's like signing my own death certificate."

"Oh, you will do what he asked you," I said, gun pointed at his head. "And I am going to give you just the right incentive to do it. Bend him over that table right there." I looked at Rico. "Pull his pants down."

I pulled a disposable camera out of my back pocket. Rico got the picture.

"Don't do this to me, man," Ronnie begged; "my manhood is all I got."

"That's why I'm taking it," I snapped. "I am going to take a few snapshots of me running up in you. If you cooperate, I will send you the negatives, and that will be the end of it. No harm, no foul. If you don't, these pictures will hit every street corner where you do business. Everyone from here to Chicago will know you as a punk-ass pillow-biter."

As I penetrated Ronnie, he began to scream like a chicken in a slaughterhouse.

It was mostly personal for me-I just wanted to feel the brown on my dick once again.

I signaled for Rico to come and get some. I knew he was thirsty as well. I also didn't want to be the only one feeding my appetite. We fucked him like "cock-aholics."

The bitch was as stunned as could be. She seemed turned on by it, too; I could see it in her eyes.

"I guess it's safe to ask where the money is

now," I said, focusing on what I really came for.

"It's in my room … in a safe behind my bed."

"Well, let's get to stepping," I insisted.

He pulled up his pants, and we headed for the bedroom.

"What's the combo?" I asked.

Ronnie reluctantly replied, "Twenty-eight right, thirty-six left, all the way around twice, then four right."

I entered the bedroom first to make sure he wasn't leading me up there to pull out a gun from the stash or some shit. True, he had on handcuffs, but you never know…

I approached the safe and put my hands to work. Like magic, the door opened for me. My eyes almost popped out of my head looking at all that cash.

"Now see, this is incentive enough for me to keep hush-hush about these flicks," I said.

"You got what you want. Take it; it's yours."

"Oh, we plan to," Rico asserted.

"Bag that shit up, Rico," I said, "so we could get the fuck out of here."

"Are you going to kill me?"

"Fuck no-I need you alive," I said. "You think I just finished digging your guts out for nothing? I'm gonna pimp you like a 'ho' on Broadway, or else…"

"Or else what?" Ronnie asked.

"Or those pictures go out-that's what. Meanwhile, don't call us," I said; "we'll call you."

We exited the bedroom.

Ronnie, too ashamed to utter a word to any-one, had the look of a woman who was just beaten and humiliated by her man.

We went to the car and made our way back to the spot.

CHAPTER FIFTEEN

Unbeknownst to me, on the other side of town, Half-a-dollar and those Gangster Unit niggers had fucked things up-apparently somebody left the gate up when I gave specific orders to pull it down. Half left it open when he went back to kill Fat Jack-another wrong move.

Little kids thought the store was open and went in and found Jack and his man dead as a doornail. The kid was banging on the glass. "Fats, hurry up. I need four quarters." He noticed the door inside the store was slightly ajar. "Fats, you in there?" he called out, sensing something was wrong. He went in and found both bodies sprawled across the floor with white mass oozing from Fat's head.

In no time police arrived on the scene. The regular police got there first, just before "supercop" and his partner.

"What do you got," Detective Hartsfield asked the detective on the scene?"

"You got one, Calvin Barnes, a.k.a. Fat Jack, and a John Doe laid out with bullets in their heads in the back of the joint."

"Any leads?" Hartsfield asked.

"Yeah," the detective answered, "a lead to nowhere. We got a clean bullet casing-probably wiped off before they got here- and a store full of fin-gerprints. Problem is: This is a game room and a candy store. We also got a couple of kids who say they haven't seen shit. I think that narrows it down to about a billion suspects in the naked city."

"Where are the kids now?"

The detective pointed to a group of kids stand-ing on the sidewalk and said, "Over there."

Hartsfield put on his best Sherlock Holmes face and walked over to the kids. "All right," he said, "which one of you want to make a crisp ten-dollar bill?"

"It all depends," one kid answered. "What we gotta do for it? No snitches over here-if that's what you mean."

"Then you must know something," said Hartsfield; "you can't snitch if you don't know noth-ing."

"Well, technically, we don't know nothing," a second kid chimed in.

"Well, not so technically, what do you know?"

The first kid signaled to the second kid. "Shut up," he said; "you talk too much."

"I don't have time for games," Hartsfield said. "I'll take all of your little asses downtown and make your mammas get out of bed to come get you. Now take this ten and gimme what I need."

That was enough for the kids to see the light.

"When we got here earlier," said one, "a guy was in front of the store giving us money, to come back later."

"Do you remember what he looked like?"

The young man held his hand to his head, trying to recall the man's face, then said, "He was dark-skinned with a scar on his mouth. We asked him about it, and he said he was shot in the mouth. We thought that was cool as shit."

"Is that it?"

"Yeah, that's it-oh yeah, he talked funny, too," the kid said. "Okay, Mr. Detective, you got twenty dollars worth of information for ten dollars."

"Then sue me," Hartsfield replied, taking a couple of steps.

The kids grabbed onto his jacket. "Detective!" one of them shouted.

"Yeah, kid."

The kid offered some more information hoping to retrieve his bounty. "One other thing: I noticed that Fats didn't have his watch on when I found him. He never took that watch off. They must have took it."

Hartsfield was salivating. "What? Was it a special kind of watch?"

"Hell yeah," he responded. "It was a Rolex flooded with diamonds."

Hartsfield went into his pocket and pulled out a twenty-dollar bill and handed it to the kid. "You see it pays to snitch sometimes," he said before getting into his car with his partner and driving off.

* * *

Meanwhile, me, Rico, and the rest of his clan were back at the spot. Half and his clique were already at the table when we got there. Money and dope was on the table. We came in with our spoils and added it to what was on the table.

Everybody sat except me. (Because I orchestrated the whole thing, most at the table saw me as a hero and leader-like I knew they would.) I was ready to make a profound speech about the event. "Behold, this is your key to liberation, your way out," I said. "As long as you keep it real with each other, you will always have it. In America, it's a fight for peace, freedom, and money. We have made war so that we may have peace. Enjoy, my niggers. Enjoy!"

They all went crazy at the table, playing with the money, lighting cigars, popping Moet, and sniffing some of the dope.

I pulled Bank to the side to discuss how everything went at Fat Jack's. "Main man," I said, "let me talk to you for a second." We both went into the back room.

He looked nervous at being singled out. "What's up?" he asked.

"Everything went down all right? Did you make sure you clipped the wires?"

"It went somewhat kosher," Bank said.

"What do you mean 'somewhat kosher'?"

"Half killed them," he blurted.

"He did what?"

"I wasn't about to argue with a nut with a loaded gun," said Bank. "He goes postal when he don't get what he wants. We should have never taken Half on this one-killing people is his passion."

I knew it was over. Something always goes wrong when you add anyone other than yourself.

"Now we all going down," I screamed, "because a motherfucker don't listen. I told y'all from the jump that if y'all listen to what I say nobody would get killed and we would all get what we wanted."

"No one saw us," Bank said.

I looked at him in amazement. I wasn't really worried, though, because my primary goal was to obtain financial resources to look out for my aunt and, if at all possible, be out of here with them to enjoy it.

"I'll make it right," I told him; "it's not your fault." And we went back into the room where everybody was dividing up the spoils.

I put on a face of happiness so as to keep them off guard. "Where's my share?" I asked. "Bag my cut so I can start living, too."

Rico handed me about seven stacks of hundred

dollar bills, which I placed in a knapsack. "You the man right now, baby." He looked at me. "I knew you could make it happen, and with Ronnie under the armpits, we got more of this coming in." He pointed to the money and the drugs."

"I'm out," I said. "I got some shit to take care of. I'll get with you later ... another day, another way."

I walked out the door and headed for my house. I knew as soon as I walked out of the door, Half would be curious as to what me and Bank were talking about.

"What did he want to talk to you about?" Half asked Bank?"

"Oh, nothing big. I told him everything went down smooth and not to worry."

"And what did he say when you told him that?" Half asked.

"He said 'all right,'" Bank responded.

*   *   *

On the way home, I saw none other than my favorite detective. (I think he had ESP or something.)

"Hey, Mr. Fraser," he said, "it's me again. I thought you might want to know-somebody just knocked off a fixture in your old 'hood."

"Why would I want to know that?"

"Because when shit falls, it falls hard. And you

204

know what?-the wrong person ends up stinking. I'm still watching you, and believe you me, if I watch a little longer, I'm going to get the answers to my problem."

*   *   *

"You ever thought for once that he might not be thinking about any wrongdoing?" Hartsfield's partner asked him as they drove off.

"Please ... he got the mark of the beast now. Once you get that first felony, society says, 'it's over,' then they commit more crimes. I'd say he was ripe for another murder. Five-he's guilty as sin-and I'm going to prove it."

"The bet is sealed. You're on."

*   *   *

I got back to the house to find my sister there, babysitting my cousin.

"Aunty just called," she told me. "She wanted to know if you were here. I told her I didn't see you since I got here."

"Did she say what she wanted?"

"No, she just wanted to speak to you, I guess,"

she said and went back to my aunt's bedroom.

I called out to her. "Wait, I have something I want to speak to you about … but first you have to promise me two things."

"What?" She looked at me crazy.

"I need your word first."

"Yes, you have my word-if you weren't my brother I would never think it."

I spat it out. "I came across a few dollars and I don't want aunty to know; I want you to look after her with it. It's not a million dollars or nothing like that, but it's enough for her to make it for a good while." I opened the bag to show her the contents.

"That's more than a few dollars-where did you get this money? Mike … tell me you're not on your way back to jail. Did you kill somebody?"

"No, not since I been home. Just promise me that whatever happens, you'll take care of aunty for me. You can even give mamma some. Put this in the room." I handed her the bag.

I had to go downstairs and catch some air. I knew if I wanted to get away with this thing I would have to get rid of Half that would definitely mean I would be back in jail for the rest of my days if I got caught. He was a loose cannon and a thorn in my side. If he got caught, the whole shit was blown, and we would all get an "accessory to murder" for his dumb-ass move.

Half and the rest of them were still at the spot, celebrating. He was fucked up as hell, talking off the wall. In his drunken stupor, was telling Rico, Young God, Bank, and the rest of them, "Your boy was too good to party with us. That motherfucking fly-by-night think he can just be in just like that, take our loot. Hell, that's my motherfucking loot-I do all the killing around this motherfucker."

"You roasted, man," Rico told him. "Go home and get some sleep."

"Fuck sleep! I'm gonna sleep when I goddam feel like sleeping."

Rico ordered someone to get Half some milk.

Half continued his tirade. "You three niggers"- he was referring to Bank, Young God, and Rico- "always undermining everybody else. Especially you, Rico. We didn't really need your man. I think it's time I assumed my position on this ship. I should be the captain."

"If that's what you want," said Rico, "then you can have it. I'm not trying to be no captain; everybody is equal. Besides, you're the only one complaining about the decision to bring Mike in."

"Y'all know he don't mean none of the shit he kicking," said Bank. "He's just torn up-that's all." Bank looked at Half. "Come on, baby boy, let's go for a walk. I'll take you to the corner store to get you some coffee and milk."

Young God and Rico held a sidebar about what just went down. "That nigger is a loose cannon," Rico said. "He's gonna get all our asses knocked."

"Ain't nobody getting knocked," Young God

said, making light of Half's tirade. "By tomorrow he's not even going to remember a word he said."

"Keep believing that!" Rico warned. "He already showed us it's all about him. He's on an ego trip. They say that when a man is drunk he always tells the truth. The sooner we realize that, the better."

Young God was still not convinced. "We'll just wait until he comes down off his high and take it from there; I want to finish partying." He held up some of the money in his hand. "We got more to be happy about than sad."

Bank was in the store across the street, trying to sober Half up with coffee and milk, and dragging him around. Bank grabbed some additional items and headed for the counter. "Here," Bank motioned to Half, "lean on this."

Half leaned on the ice freezer, his hands stretched out over it.

Detective Hartsfield came in the store to get coffee and greeted the cashier, "Hey, Arty, what you know good? Business slow tonight?"

"Not since you walked in," Arty joked. "How's the missus? She throw you out yet?"

"No, not yet," Hartsfield said, walking to the counter to pay for the donut and coffee. "Nice watch!"-He noticed the watch on Half's wrist, the dia-monds-"What-you hit the lottery?"

"Your mother bought it for me!" Half snapped,

obviously still fucked up.

Bank knew he was in deep shit. It never even dawned on him that Half had on Fat Jack's watch. "You'll have to excuse him," Bank apologized; "he's a little tipsy-that's all."

"You can say that again," said Hartsfield. "Let's see if downtown can take him off his toes and put him on his feet." Hartsfield signaled for his partner.

"There's no need for that, officer. I can get in a cab with him and see to it that he gets in his house."

Hartsfield knew this was the opportunity of a lifetime. "I bet you can," he said, "but just to be on the safe side, I think I better take him in. I couldn't live with myself if he stumbled and bust his head or something."

Hartsfield handcuffed Half and took him to the precinct and charged him with public drunkenness ... to legally hold him in custody.

Bank ran back to the spot to let everyone know that Half had just been arrested. Out of breath, he knocked on the door, and Rico answered and opened up for him.

"They got Half!" Bank yelled.

"Who?" asked Rico.

Everybody was aroused now, listening intently.

"Five-O. He was acting up when we was in the store and a knocker came in and took him downtown. He was asking about a watch Half had on. I think he took that shit from Jack. I didn't even notice it. We got to go get him out of there ... before they find out about the watch."

"Calm down, motherfucker," Rico demanded. "First things first: What watch?-I know you ain't talking about nothing taken from where we said don't take nothing from."

Rico grabbed him and threw him against the wall. They knew they had to get down to the precinct before this nigger started acting like a parrot.

*   *   *

At the precinct, Hartsfield was bombarding Half with a ton of questions. "Talk to me, you murdering son-of-a-bitch. Give me what I need to know and you can go in that cell and sleep all day if you want to. I've seen your kind before; I've been on the job a long time."

"All I know is I didn't kill anybody," Half responded, not yet out of his stupor

"Go right ahead. What are you implying-you know who did?"

"I ain't say that, but your boy, good ol' Mr. Fraser might know something."

"You mean Michael Fraser?"

"You said it; I didn't. You do the math. I heard he already got a murder charge for sticking up somebody. As soon as he gets home, shit starts around here-at least, that's what I hear. I ain't from around here, so I don't know everything."

"Come on, son. Work with me. You got the watch; you gonna have to come up with a little more than-"

"Oh shit!"

Hartsfield, interrupted by Half's outburst, turned around just in time to see Rico and Young God enter the precinct.

"Look, I didn't tell you anything!" Half whispered.

"Hold tight. Keep your panties on," Hartsfield said.

Rico and YG looked at Half suspiciously.

"How may I help you boys?" asked Hartsfield.

"You can help us by letting us know if you charging our boy with anything so we can meet you at the courthouse with bail," said Rico, with a look of disdain.

"Now, now, now ..." said Hartsfield, fearful things might slip away from him, "... don't go sending your boy downtown in front of a judge before his time; you'll all have a turn at that."

"And what the fuck that's suppose to mean?" Young God asked angrily.

"I'm just calling it like I see it-but that's another story. I'm not going to hold him; I think he's sobered up rather nicely. As for you future convicts, I suggest you stay the fuck away from Mr. Fraser."

Rico wasn't trying to hear the rhetoric. "Is he free to go or what?"

"Yeah, he's free to go. As free as a bird in the sky."

"Thank you, overseer-I mean officer," said Young God, as he, Rico, and Half headed out.

Before they got to the door Hartsfield said to Half, "Thanks for everything," and winked at him like some bitch.

Outside, "A touch of class" was waiting for them. Bank was already inside the car in the backseat with Young God; Half was in the middle. Rico sat in the front.

"Seems like you was having a pretty good conversation," Rico said to Half. "I almost didn't want to interrupt."

"Fuck you! What? I look like a snitch to you? Who the fuck am I going to snitch on? Myself?"

"You said it," Rico shot back; "I didn't."

Just as Half noticed they were driving towards the water, Rico put the automatic lock on the doors.

"Why are we going this way?" Half asked. "I know we not going to pick up no work with all of us in here!"

Rico smiled at Young God. "Ain't nobody picking up nothing; we going to drop something off."

"We got work in the car?" Half asked.

"Ain't no work in this ride," Rico said, "but this joint is definitely dirty as a motherfucker."

"I know y'all don't think I told," Half said frantically. "Oh shit, it's like that. That's how y'all motherfuckers going out?"

As Half reached for the door, Rico spotted a police car in his rearview mirror and calmly looked back at Bank and Young God and said, "Five-O right behind us." Then he turned up the music and cracked the window slightly. "Just start singing and clapping to the song."

The cops moved up alongside them while the light was on red, looked at Rico, and gave him a sign to turn the music down some before driving off.

Half tried to get their attention, but the sound of the music drowned him out.

Rico gave the officer a thumbs up, and breathed a heavy sigh of relief when the cops moved on.

The cop in the passenger seat looked at his partner and said, "That car is too noisy for them to be guilty of doing anything; you can hear them coming a mile away."

When they reached the Westside Highway, right by the water, they all got out of the car. Rico reached under the seat for a .45.

"Yo, Bank, you my nigger," Half pleaded. "You going to let these niggers fade me?"

"I wash my hands of it," Bank said. "You out of control now; you don't listen to nobody!"

"Nobody is going to fade you; you gonna fade yourself," Rico told him. "I'm gonna give you a chance to run like hell."

"Then what?" Half figured there was a catch.

"Then nothing."

"If you was going to let me run, why you brought me over here then?"

"Because this is your track." Rico pointed toward the Hudson. "You can either sink or swim; at least you have a chance at life."

Half looked at the water-"All right then ... if this is how it got to be"-grabbed Bank, interlocking their arms, and pulling them backwards into the river-"we'll see you in hell, nigger!"

Rico tried to grab Bank but was too late. Bank held onto a log at the base of the dock and was dragged under by the current yelling, "Somebody help me! Help!"

Rico dropped a long piece of railing pipe in the water to try and save him, but the thick current swept him away.

CHAPTER SIXTEEN

Seven months had passed since the incident at the river. I was spending money like crazy.

Those two detectives were also on my ass-I couldn't breathe-following me around and shit.

Rico and Young God were still gambling, staying in the game. I backed off from both of them, deciding to count my blessings and make good on the paper I had.

Diane had hit me with some news that brought tears of joy to my eyes: She was pregnant, due to give birth at the end of the year. Life was really looking up in spite of all the shit I was dealing with.

We decided to invest in property in Baltimore, Maryland where we would raise our child. By all accounts, I was on my way to achieving the American dream-without the help of the system.

Everything was going great, except for my health. I was feeling sluggish all the time and was losing a lot of weight. My eyes started to sink in, and my mouth was always dry. Everyone was telling me to go to the doctor, but I wasn't trying to hear that. I had no time for bad news; I was trying to do things.

I was pretty confident that Hartsfield would meet a dead end trying to pin anything on me; that was the least of my worries. Rico and Young God had covered most of the tracks, and I had no reason to believe either of them would ever rat me out. I figured they were going to be murdered in the game before they could even get a chance to say anything … if they wanted to.

Meanwhile, I was hanging out with the two homos from the salon, Precious and Toni, on a regular basis, sneaking with them over the 135th Street Bridge to the Quarry, an exclusive fag joint. I used to enter the club as if I was looking for them, to give them something. The bouncers would let me in, and I would never come out.

The atmosphere there was always loose and crazy, but I kept going back. In the bathrooms, men used to engage in all types of fucking and sucking. Men were in stalls abusing themselves, face-fucking each other tag-team, and baby dykes could be seen fondling each other.

Behind the DJ booth, men chain-fucked each other while others had "cum-drinking" contests. There was the pearl necklace contest, sausage jockey king, ball-banging contest, and commitment ceremonies taking place. They also kept small parties in selected areas of the club for "new converts."

Precious and Toni always introduced me as a "friend of Dorothy,"-which meant I wasn't a homo but was tolerant of the lifestyle-to protect my image on the street. I told them, "If I was going to be hanging out with y'all, the last thing I want was some fag coming up to me on the street and putting me on "broad street" in front of everyone."

I also had my girl's feelings to protect; after all I was about to be a father.

There was something about being a father that brought new life to my being. It was a way in which I could start life all over through my little man's life, to rekindle the hope that was lost in my life.

I got a call from Diane the night before a monthly check-up. She was bleeding from her nose profusely and wanted to go to the hospital. She told me to meet her at Harlem Hospital-in the emergency room. I didn't know what to think.

When I got there, doctors were poking her arm and taking blood. Her blood pressure was exceedingly low; they thought she might have been going into premature labor, so they ushered her upstairs to the delivery room.

Other doctors were talking on the side as if there was more to it.

I wanted some answers fast. One of the attending doctors called me into a small room. "Have a seat," he said.

I just knew something was very wrong.

"Mr. Fraser," he said, "you're the father of this child, correct?"

"Yes, I am."

"I am sorry, but I have some bad news concerning your child and his mother." He opened up the chart that was in front of him. "I don't know how we didn't pick it up before, but it seems that your fiancée is suffering from an advanced stage of HIV. There is also a strong possibility that your child is infected as well. We didn't want to tell her in her present condition.

"Her immune system is almost shut down, leaving her and the child vulnerable to various infections. Her chronic bleeding is a result of an attack on her blood cells. You-or she-will have to make a choice as to what should be done … if we can only save one of them. The decision is up to both of you-I thought it should be you to tell her.

"We don't have much time, so you will have to act fast. We also need a blood sample from you as well."

If there ever was a time I felt like the world was coming to an end it was now. What in the world did I do to deserve this? More importantly, what did Diane or my child do to deserve this? How could I tell the mother of my child that she was suffering from a deadly illness, delivering her only child?

Then it all started to make sense. I was feeling sick and sluggish because my body was telling me something. And I didn't want to hear. I had gotten it from Dee Dee and passed it on to Diane without even knowing.

The doctor didn't have to make the call; I knew

what I had to do.

I went upstairs to the delivery room and faced my demons. I had no choice but to tell her ... as she lay on the table in pain.

Her contractions were less than two minutes apart, and the doctors feared the worst. I looked at her eyes and ran back outside the delivery room when the tears began to roll down my face. I didn't have the strength to tell her.

For the first time in my life I felt love and compassion-she was the mother of my child.

The doctor was making his way into the delivery room when I approached him. "Doc, can I talk to you for a second?"

"Sure, but make it quick. They just called me from downstairs to tell me that she was ready to have the baby. Did you talk to her yet?"

"No, I haven't, but I've decided to make the decision for her. I love her dearly, and I love my first-born more than you will ever know. I want you to save her, doc-at all cost. I'll sign whatever I have to sign. I can have another child, but there will only be one Diane."

The doctor looked at me as if he agreed with my decision. I knew if I told her she would have preferred to die and save her child. But I had ruined her life, so the least I could do was to let her enjoy whatever was left.

With every passing minute I could hear the screams of labor intensify. I couldn't bear to go in-that meant looking her in the face and concealing my deceit.

After eight exhausting hours, the doctor came out of the delivery room with his head hung down. "Mr. Fraser," he said, "I'm sorry, we couldn't save the baby."

I kind of figured that, even though I was hoping for a miracle.

"I am afraid I have more bad news," he added. "We weren't able to save your fiancée either. There was just too much blood loss. The baby wrapped itself around the umbilical cord, making it difficult to control the bleeding or get him out before he suffocated."

I was speechless.

I went into that room with the weight of the world on my shoulders. Two lifeless bodies lay on a slab, left for dead.

My boy looked just like me. I named him Michael Jr.; after all, he was a full-blown baby, deserving of a name and a decent funeral.

Diane's eyes were wide open. She had the look of disappointment, like she'd been let down by my absence when she took her last breath. She died for no reason at all-other than my stupidity.

There was no way I could face her family at a funeral. Being there would only make it worse, I thought. I looked upon her face and my child's one last time before exiting the delivery room.

I walked out of there with a new outlook on

life and a new way of sharing it-I was going to be honest with myself and others, and come out of the closet.

*   *   *

I'd made up my mind to check with my parole officer-he'd been looking for me for violating my cur- few-to finish up the thirteen months I owed the sys- tem.

I called Precious and Toni and told them I was "going in" the following morning and made them an offer to wait for me until I got out, so we could all make a move together to Baltimore and open a unisex salon of our own.

*   *   *

If Dee Dee didn't do anything else for me, she sure brought me out. Funny how things worked out, I thought. I was just so sorry I had to lose two people to find that out.

See y'all in Baltimore!

This book is dedicated to the most important woman in my life. Patricia Dyan Harris, you have stuck by me when the world left me for dead. We have been through a lot together and at times you get me sick. I am sure I make you sick more than a little bit, but you manage to see past my faults and all the bullshit and love me just the same. I also want to thank you for not judging me for writing this book.

Undoubtedly my sexuality will be questioned for writing this book; I can live with it because I know I am not a Homo. I have learned that a person in that type of lifestyle can't hide it-the very nature of being gay makes them expose who they are, and who they've been with. If I was gay, trust me, the world would know about it because they would tell it. I have no skeletons in my closet.

Back to you, sweetie: Thanks for believing in the vision. I just felt like it was a story that deserved to be told and I should be the one to tell it.

Pat, I can go on and on about how much you mean to me. The bottom line is, all of those bitches, including people in your family, who said our relationship was built on bullshit, are presently out of one and lonely as hell. We are still together. To all of them I say, "Eat a dick up until you hiccup!"

OTHER BOOKS BY ASANTE KAHARI:

THE BIRTH OF A CRIMINAL
PRINCIPLES OF THE GAME
THOUGHTS OF A BLACKMAN and
MURDER INC.